The Truth Twisters

The Truth Twisters

A NOVELPLUS

Josh McDowell
& Bob Hostetler

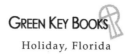

Green Key Books
Holiday, Florida

THE TRUTH TWISTERS

ISBN: 1932587845

Cover graphics: Kirk DouPonce, dogeareddesign.com

Project Management by JJ Graphics

Library of Congress Cataloging-in-Publication Data available upon request.

Published by Green Key Books
2514 Aloha Place
Holiday, FL 34691

Editorial assistance provided by The Livingstone Corporation (www.LivingstoneCorp.com). Project staff includes Linda Taylor and Dawn Jett.

Printed in the United States of America.

06 07 08 09 5 4 3 2 1

Table of Contents

CHAPTER ONE

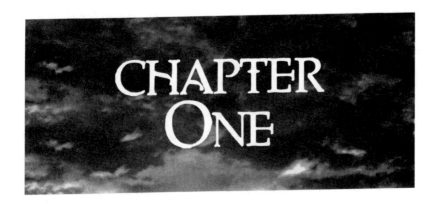

Jessica woke screaming. She opened her eyes into the darkness and clawed at the air, gasping for breath. She thrashed against the sheets and bedspread as if imprisoned, as if they impeded her escape.

Blind with terror, gulping great drafts of air, she would have climbed to the ceiling if her hands could have found anything to grasp. But the darkness was stronger than she was, swallowing her, dragging her back down, helplessly, hopelessly . . .

Suddenly she felt something wrap itself tightly around her. She struggled against it, desperate to break free. Pulling her flailing arms close to her body, she groped to find a grip on the thing that was tightening around her, preventing her escape to light, air, life. She shrieked louder, now with fury along with fear, tucking her chin into her chest, gnashing her teeth, hoping to find something to bite into so she could tear free.

"Jessica," the thing called into her darkness. Her own screams were now mingled with the shouts of another. It was a voice she knew, a voice that confused her, stopped the screams in her throat, and left her heaving, panting, sobbing . . . but no longer fighting.

The panic ebbed, and her sobbing slowed. Air entered her lungs now in short gasps.

"It's me, sweetheart. It's your mother."

Jessica slowly became aware of her surroundings.

The room was no longer dark.

"You're awake now," her mother said. "You're safe. I'm here."

Jessica wilted like a flower and laid her head on her mother's shoulder, whimpering and sobbing. Her mother stroked her hair and rocked her back and forth on the bed as if she were an infant instead of a sixteen year old. She lay against her mother for a long time, exhausted, depleted, unspeakably sad.

Finally, her mother shifted and pushed Jessica's limp form up off her shoulder. "That's the second time this week, sweetheart."

With great effort, Jessica lifted her head and shoulders and looked at her mother through eyes still clouded with tears. "I know," she answered. She started to cry again.

"I don't know what to do for you."

"I know," Jessica said. "I don't know, either."

"They're not getting any better, are they?"

Jessica shook her head.

"Are they getting worse?"

She wiped a tear from her cheek with her hand. She shrugged. "I don't know. Maybe."

"Do you want to sleep in my room the rest of the night? I wouldn't mind the company, you know. It gets awful lonely in there."

Jessica attempted a smile. "Thanks," she said, "but I could never go back to sleep now. I think I'll just stay up."

Her mom nodded and flashed a joyless smile. "Me, too. We'll just go downstairs and raid the refrigerator. I could bake some cookies. How would you like that? It would be fun."

Jessica rose from her bed. She opened her closet door and took out her robe. She slipped it over her shoulders and pulled her long blond hair out from under the robe's collar. She shook her head. "I'll be fine, Mom. You go back to bed."

They exchanged glances. Neither moved.

"You have to go to work in the morning," Jessica said. "All I have to do is start getting ready for the church mission trip. I can take a nap on the couch if I need to, but you should go back to bed."

Her mother stood and sighed. "You're sure you'll be okay?"

Jessica nodded without meeting her mother's gaze. "Yeah," she said. She just didn't believe it.

† † † † † † †

Shawn felt the dirt bike shudder beneath him. He knew he was perilously close to losing control, but he wasn't about to let Ryan win this one. The path looked like it narrowed ahead, and he saw his chance.

"Think I can't pass you there?" he muttered through clenched teeth. "Watch me."

He throttled the bike and felt it lurch forward, fishtailing from the sudden change in momentum. He saw Ryan's head turn slightly and guessed that he was gauging Shawn's location. He feinted as though he were preparing to pass on the left where the path dropped suddenly off the side of the hill. Instead, he swerved quickly to Ryan's right and pointed his bike between Ryan and the face of the cliff.

His elbow scraped the sharp rock of the hillside, but instead of slowing, he opened the throttle a little more. In the split second that he pulled even with Ryan, he saw a brief look of disbelief on his friend's face. He grinned with satisfaction before pulling away and leaning into the narrowest part of the trail to prevent Ryan from maneuvering around him.

He'd done it! He'd pulled it off! He was sick and tired of Ryan's smug comment after every ride: "I could have passed you if I wanted to." This time, as they mounted their bikes at the trail head, Shawn had poked a finger into his friend's chest and said, "I'm going to let you go first, and I'm going to pass you whether you like it or not."

And so he had. He swiveled in his seat to gloat a little over his victory, but Ryan wasn't there. He had disappeared from the trail.

A sick feeling suddenly clenched Shawn's gut. He slowed and stopped, turning sideways on his seat to look back down the path. He tried to listen over the purr of his idled engine for the sound of Ryan's bike approaching, but he heard nothing. He turned around and slowly, carefully headed back toward the spot where he had passed his friend.

"If he's dead, God . . ." he started, correcting himself immediately. "Please don't let him be dead. Please let him be okay." He kicked himself mentally. *Always taking chances. Always taking it too far, aren't you? Always.*

He was still kicking himself moments later when he arrived back at the narrow bend where he had passed Ryan just minutes earlier. Immediately, he saw the skid marks leading off the side of the hill. His heart seemed to rise up from his chest and fill his throat. He opened his mouth, wanting to call Ryan's name, but he couldn't make a noise.

He stepped to the edge where the path dropped off and peered over the steep drop. For a moment all he saw was air and rock and the ground far below. Then he saw Ryan and heard his bike at the same moment.

Ryan still sat on his bike, maneuvering it slowly up the side of the hill. There was no path, no trail, but Ryan steered the bike over rocks and clumps of grass. Shawn watched with relief as his friend finally made it back to the trail and straddled the bike while he inspected the scrapes and cuts from his fall.

Shawn pulled parallel to Ryan, who looked up at him without smiling.

"You jerk," Ryan said.

His tone reassured Shawn, a little. "Yeah," he agreed. He opened his mouth to apologize, but Ryan spoke first.

"You go ahead," Ryan said, nodding up the trail. "I want to be able to see you for the rest of the ride."

Shawn didn't argue. He would finish the ride in the lead, but without feeling a sense of victory . . . only emptiness. As usual.

† † † † † † †

"Is this the best you can do?"

Shawn hadn't even shut the door behind him when his dad met him in the entryway of the large Westcastle home where he lived with his parents and older sister. He quickly recognized the piece of paper in his father's hand. Apparently his final grades from the school year had arrived in the mail that day.

"Hi, Dad," he said.

"When are you going to wake up?" Mr. Lee said.

Shawn sighed as he kicked off his shoes and shut the door. "I know," he said. He knew exactly where this conversation was going.

"No, you don't know. Your mother and I have tried everything we can think of to help you succeed. We've tried grounding you. We've tried rewarding you on those rare occasions when you do something right. We've tried counseling—everything! But all you seem to care about is going to concerts, riding dirt bikes, staying out late, and having a good time. You're seventeen years old, Shawn! When are you going to wake up and start acting like it?"

Shawn didn't meet his father's angry gaze. He knew his father, whose parents were hardworking Asian immigrants, believed in education more than almost anything. Shawn thrust his hands into his pockets.

"I've had it," his father said. He flung the paper at Shawn's chest, but it took a sharp turn toward the floor. He spun on his heel and walked away, shaking his head.

Shawn stood for a few moments in the entryway, his hands in his pockets. His grades stared up at him from the floor. He thought about picking up the paper but stepped over it and went upstairs to his room, where he picked up the phone and pressed redial.

"Is Jessica there?" he asked. He paused, listening to the voice on the other end of the line. "Oh yeah," he said after a few moments. "Bible study. I forgot."

† † † † † † †

FAR BELOW the town of Westcastle, in the smoky, sulfurous caverns of hell, a grotesque figure cursed the darkness.

"How's a demon supposed to tie a bow tie in this infernal darkness?" the figure croaked. He faced the oozing, slug-covered wall of the dank cavern and fumbled before the outline of his own image in a musty mirror. His slimy, frog-like fingers repeatedly failed him as he tried to form something resembling a formal bow tie around his rubbery neck.

His name was Ratsbane, and like all demons of hell, he inhabited an ugly mutant body—a cruel, twisted joke perpetrated by Satan on his joyless followers, the angels who eons ago had rebelled against the God of heaven and earth and so lost their heavenly position, power, and beauty. Ratsbane occupied the wart-covered carcass of a gigantic toad, topped with an even more ridiculous oversized head of a carpenter ant. The proportions of his head—combined with the gloom that surrounded him—made the task of tying a formal bow tie almost impossible.

"Nefarius!" he screamed, though the sound emitted was the belch of a bullfrog. He threw up his frog hands in frustration and whirled. "Nefarius!" he called again, peering hard into the murky cavern with his bulbous ant eyes.

He smelled his demon assistant before he saw him. The creature had always smelled like a zoo, but his recent stints in the sulfur pits and slag heaps of hell—banished there by Ratsbane himself as revenge for having attempted to usurp Ratsbane's prime position as Foreman of Subsector 1122—had made Nefarius the foulest-smelling fiend since the legendary Legion. Ratsbane had rescued him from banishment, not out of kindness (for no evil spirit can summon such a virtue), but because his more recent assistants and associates had all betrayed and deserted Ratsbane (as demons are expected and encouraged to do).

Nefarius finally turned the corner and entered Ratsbane's dim vision. The under-demon inhabited a gorilla's body, with hair tangled and matted as though he had rolled around in a garbage heap like a puppy in a meadow (which, in fact, he occasionally did). His demon eyes looked out from the head of a walrus, with one of his yellowed tusks broken jaggedly in half.

"Yes, Your Malevolence?" Nefarious sneered through his tusk-and-a-half.

"Tie this," Ratsbane barked. "And be quick about it. I'm going to be late for the ceremony."

Nefarius reached for the thing around Ratsbane's neck and gathered up each end into a grubby gorilla paw. "What is it?"

"It's a bow tie, you worthless pile of sewer sludge."

Nefarius tugged the two ends, crossing his hands under the mandibles that protruded from Ratsbane's mouth. He pulled them tight, then even tighter, leaning forward and peering into one of his superior's vacant obsidian eyes. He held on for a moment then loosened his grip, letting the ends of the tie drop.

"I don't know how to tie a bow tie," he said.

"You were choking me!" Ratsbane gasped, grabbing at his neck with both webbed hands.

"I don't think it's big enough," Nefarius said nonchalantly.

"Not big enough to fit? Or not big enough to choke me with?" Ratsbane demanded.

"Yes," Nefarius answered.

"You're a treacherous good-for-nothing!" Ratsbane croaked, ripping the tie off and tossing it to the cold stone floor.

"Thank you," Nefarius answered.

✝✝✝✝✝✝✝

(THE INSIDE STORY)
BUT WAIT . . . THERE'S MORE!

You've seen them. They're called infomercials. Most of the time you just skip over them as you're flipping television channels looking for your favorite show. But every once in a while, you stop and watch for a few minutes.

How much would you expect to pay for the HomeComfort Spa and Wave Pool? Twenty thousand dollars? Ten thousand? But wait . . . there's more!

If you order today, we'll include an extreme makeover—including surgery—absolutely free of charge! That's right, you can lose those fifty pounds you gained last Christmas. Or get rid of those unsightly bald spots. Or have your whole face removed and replace it with the face of your favorite movie star! But wait . . . there's more!

If you call right now, 1-800-Swindle (that's 1-800-794-6353), we will send you a fully-functioning airplane large enough to seat four adults—yet it folds in just seconds and fits into your purse or wallet. Never worry about airline schedules or airport security again. It's the ultimate in twenty-first century travel. And it's yours if you call and order now!

"But wait . . . there's more!" Such claims can get pretty ridiculous. In this case, it's actually true. This book really does offer more than most. It's called a NovelPlus, a concept created specifically for the Powerlink Chronicles (*Under Siege, The Love Killer, Truth Slayers, The Deceivers,* and this book). You've already been introduced to a couple of the characters in this book, Jessica Furman and Shawn Lee. You'll also meet other characters, members of the Westcastle Community Church youth group, including Duane and Liz Cunningham, Westcastle's youth pastors, who have been featured in every one of the Powerlink Chronicles to date.

But wait . . . there's more. Not only will you follow the story of Jessica and Shawn and the Westcastle group, you'll also follow another story line depicting the workings of a demonic underworld. You've already met Ratsbane and his assistant Nefarius, but you haven't yet discovered the diabolical strategy advancing in the lives of the Westcastle kids. These occasional glimpses into the caves and corridors of hell will not only reveal what evil the forces of darkness are perpetrating on the Westcastle kids, they will also expose the strategy Satan is trying to use on you and your generation to create the same kind of emptiness and frustration that Jessica and Shawn are struggling with.

But wait . . . there's more. The third dimension of this book is in sections called "The Inside Story." We will interrupt the fiction at key points and present important insights or explanations of things that are going on in the novel, helping you also to apply that understanding to similar things that happen in your life. These insights are so important that, while you may be tempted to skip ahead to see what happens next in the story, we urge you not to give in to that temptation. The content of these sections will make later developments in Jessica and Shawn's story much easier to follow and will also help you more fully understand and apply the concepts of this book to your own life.

CHAPTER TWO

Jessica sat cross-legged on the floor while her mother busied herself in the kitchen. Six other girls sat around the room, two on the floor, three on the couch, and one in the chair next to Jessica. Two plates of cookies were on the table in the center of the room. She held an open Bible on her lap, waiting for the right time to start the Bible study she had been leading for almost three months.

"Isn't it *so* exciting," Bethany gushed, not directing her comments to anyone in particular, "that Sarah Milford gets to pray at graduation? I wonder if she's nervous. I know I would be."

Anna scribbled furiously in her journal, as if she would forget it all if she didn't write it down as fast as possible.

Alison's face displayed an expression of mild curiosity about everything going on around her. "Is there more food in the kitchen?" she asked Jessica. "You know, in case this isn't enough."

Jessica nodded and smiled at Alison. "There's plenty. You know my mom."

Shannon lifted her hand slightly and then put it back in her lap as though she had forgotten that she wasn't in school and didn't have to raise her hand in order to talk. "Does everybody know that Andy Matthews was in a car accident last night?"

Several of the girls responded with surprise, and Shannon continued. "He's all right, I guess. My dad talked to his dad, and he may have a broken rib, but it could just be bruised."

"We need to pray," Bethany said. "We should all pray for Andy right now."

Jessica shifted in her chair and reached out her hands. The first time she'd led this Bible study—she'd never even been in a Bible study before this one—she had asked the girls to hold hands when they prayed. It had become a custom of sorts; they'd done it every time since.

The girls joined hands and bowed their heads. Jessica prayed briefly, asking God to bless their study and to pay special attention to Andy Matthews. She closed by asking him to help each of them to get something special out of their time together. When she said "amen," the girls dropped their hands and then sighed slightly as if they'd been holding their breath together.

"Does anyone remember what we studied last week?" Jessica asked the group.

"Moses," Alison said.

"Yes," agreed Jessica slowly. They'd been studying the story of Moses for months. "Do you remember anything else?"

No one answered quickly. After a few moments of silence, Anna spoke without taking her eyes off the journal in her lap. "We talked about the thirty-third chapter of Exodus. God talks to Moses up on Mount Sinai. Moses asks God not to leave Israel but to stick with them, even though they have sinned. God hides Moses in the cleft of the rock and lets him see his back as he passes by."

The whole group gazed respectfully at Anna as she finished summarizing the previous week's study. Alison smiled and nodded enthusiastically, as if Anna had simply repeated what she had meant to say.

"Right," Jessica said. "Tonight we're going to study Exodus thirty-four." She opened her Bible, and the other girls dutifully turned the pages of their Bibles to the chapter. Jessica asked Bethany to read the first seven verses aloud while the others followed along in their own Bibles.

When Bethany finished reading, Jessica looked up from her Bible and said, "What do those verses mean *to you*?"

No one answered right away. Shannon eventually spoke. "I think, to me, it's like that saying, 'If at first you don't succeed, try, try again.' My dad says that a lot."

Jessica nodded. "Okay, sure," she said. "What about the rest of you? What do those verses mean *to you*?"

Anna stopped writing. "Can we talk a little about what was actually *on* the stone tablets Moses was supposed to carve?"

"Okay, sure," Jessica said. "What do you *think* was on them?"

Anna blinked at Jessica, her mouth hanging open. "Well, I'm sure those stone things had actual words on them. And I guess God really meant something when he wrote them. Shouldn't we try to find out exactly what they were and what he meant?"

"Well," replied Jessica, "the Bible is meant for us to use in our own lives, isn't it? I mean, like when you have a problem or something, you can go to the Bible, find good words of wisdom there, and use that wisdom in a way that works to fit your needs. Your needs will be different from mine, so the meaning you get from the Bible may be different from the meaning I get."

"It's like the truth you get from the Bible may be different from the truth I get, right?" said Shannon.

"Yeah, that's the idea," agreed Jessica. "Each of us has to find the truth for ourselves inside ourselves. We sort of find it by exploring our own needs and experiences. I can't make your truth; you can't make mine. There's not just one truth for all of us, but each of us can use the Bible to help us find the truth that's right for us."

"That means what God is like is a little different for each one of us, I think," said Shannon.

"I think to me," Alison said, "God's like everybody's father, you know?"

Anna looked at Alison with a puzzled expression and then looked at Jessica again. She wasn't buying into all this, but she didn't know how to refute it. Shannon agreed. "My mom used to say *all* the time, 'Wait till your father gets home!'"

"What it means to me," Jessica offered, "is that God loves us, but he has to punish us whenever we do something wrong. We can never measure up to his standards, so even though he doesn't want to, he has to punish us when we fail so we can learn to do better." A self-conscious silence followed Jessica's remarks. A few of the girls wrinkled their foreheads in thought. Anna's face still wore a quizzical look, and Alison drew swirls with her finger in the carpet where she sat. "That," added Jessica, "is what it means to me."

✝✝✝✝✝✝✝

Shawn slipped downstairs as quietly as he could, not wanting to run into his father again. He knew his father wasn't done yelling at him for his grades, but there was no need to get in his way right now. His grade report was still on the floor where he left it. He picked it up and shoved it into his pocket before quietly slipping out the front door.

He jumped into his car. A taillight was still missing from a rainy night a few weeks ago when he had fishtailed on Nichols Road and spun off the pavement, taking a street sign into the ditch with him. He knew he'd been going too fast as he approached the *S* curve, but he couldn't slow down for every turn in the road. He didn't like to scratch or ding up his car, but he could always fix it later when he had the money.

He frowned at his own thoughts as he pulled away from his house. His dad was wrong, dead wrong. Shawn didn't care about the things his dad said— "going to concerts, riding dirt bikes, staying out late, and having a good time." He didn't care about much of anything. He didn't care about hurting himself. He didn't care about money. He didn't care if he passed his junior year. He didn't care if his parents thought he was a loser.

Jessica was a different matter, however. He cared about her. They'd been dating for months, and he couldn't get her off his mind. He'd dated other girls in the past, but after a few weeks or a couple months, he would tire of the relationship. But he had not tired of Jessica.

His car tires squealed as he took the sharp turn off Hudson onto Becker. "I've never felt this way about another girl," he said, rehearsing what he planned to say to Jessica. "I think you feel the same way about me—"

A brown and white beagle suddenly dashed into the street in front of the car. Shawn yanked the steering wheel hard to the left . . . and into the path of an approaching white panel van.

† † † † † † †

Alison helped Jessica finish straightening the room after the other girls left the Bible study. She picked up a couple cushions from the floor and tossed them onto the couch while Jessica moved her mom's favorite chair back to its usual place.

"Are you packed for the trip?" Alison asked.

Jessica picked up her Bible from the floor. She shook her head. "No," she said slowly, "not really."

"You need help? I could help you. I'm all packed. I've been packed for three days now. All I have to do is put my toothbrush in the suitcase because I only have one toothbrush. My mom wanted to buy a new one, but I like the one I have now, you know?"

Jessica nodded and smiled.

"So, do you?" Alison asked.

"Do I . . . what? Like the toothbrush I have now?"

"Do you need help packing? I wouldn't mind at all. It would be fun, you know?"

Jessica shrugged. "No, that's okay. I think my mom wants to help me."

Alison wore a disappointed look for a moment, but her expression brightened again quickly. "I bet it's going to be hard spending almost two weeks without Shawn, huh? I mean, if I had a boyfriend—which I haven't for almost the whole year because the boys who ask me out aren't the ones I want to ask me out, you know? But if I had a boyfriend, I think it would be hard to go off to Africa without him, even though it's only two weeks, but two weeks can seem like forever sometimes."

"Yeah . . ."

Alison left a few minutes later. She was still talking as she closed the door of Jessica's house behind her. Jessica stood in the front entryway, still hugging her Bible against her chest. *It should be hard to go off to Africa without Shawn,* she told herself, *but it's not. It's going to be a relief.*

She stared at the door. She and Shawn had been a couple for more than six months. At first she thought he would be just what she wanted, what she needed to fill the emptiness inside her. Why was it so hard to fill that emptiness? She was really trying. She had searched her heart and soul for the solution, for an answer she was sure she could find within herself if she just kept trying. She thought using wisdom from the Bible would help her find it, but she just felt emptier and more confused as week after week passed by. In recent weeks, her relationship with Shawn had become more physical, and she was plagued with guilt and shame for some of the things they had done together.

I can't keep doing this, she told herself. *I have to break it off with Shawn. I know God doesn't like it, and if I don't do something soon, he's going to punish me.* A shudder ran up her spine, and she tightened her crossed arms around her Bible. Maybe she didn't know what caused the emptiness in her life, but she knew that she understood God. He was loving, yes, but uncompromising when it came to doing right. He was always watching, ready to bring people back in line with his discipline. The way she and Shawn had been giving in to their physical feelings showed her that the relationship was wrong. God would not approve, and sooner or later he would have to administer his discipline. *I've got to break it off with Shawn now. I won't put it off any longer. I can't wait until I get back from Africa. I have to tell him. I have to.*

A sudden rap on the door startled her, and she felt like she had just jumped a foot into the air. She lifted a hand to her mouth and tried to catch her breath. After a moment, she reached for the doorknob.

Shawn stood outside the door on her front porch.

Jessica blinked at him in surprise. "What are you doing here?"

"I just about got killed on the way over here," he said. Jessica stepped aside and Shawn entered. "A dog jumped out in front of me. I swerved to miss it and almost got hit head-on by a van." He held his hand out in front of him and Jessica could see that it shook slightly. "What a rush!" he grinned.

She closed the door. "What are you doing here?" she repeated.

"Why, what's wrong?" he said.

She shook her head. "Nothing. I just didn't expect to see you tonight. I just finished the girls' Bible study."

He nodded. "I know. I tried to call."

"Why?"

"I wanted to talk to you."

They stared at each other through a few moments of silence. Finally, Jessica said, "Okay. Sure."

"Is your mom home?" he asked.

"She's upstairs." Jessica turned and headed for the kitchen. "Do you want something to drink?"

"No," he said. "Listen." He touched her elbow, and they stopped in the center of the living room. He made a few awkward attempts to say what was on his mind, amazed at how dry his throat had suddenly become. Eventually, however, he managed to get to the point. "I—I've never felt the way I feel about you," he said. "I mean, I've never felt this way about anyone else before. And I think—at least, I hope—I mean, I think maybe you sort of feel the same way, too, and—well, I just think it's time that we, you know, take our relationship to a new level."

She blinked her surprise at him. "What do you mean?"

"I don't mean get married," he blurted. "I just think we're ready to get more serious. I want to get you a ring."

"A ring?"

"Not an engagement ring!" He held his hands up like a cop stopping traffic. He licked his lips as though his mouth was suddenly dry. "I mean, just a ring. You know, to say that we're serious. Like we're committed to each other."

She held her Bible to her chest as though she were clinging to a life preserver. "Committed."

"Yeah," he said. "I—Don't you think we're ready for that?"

She looked everywhere but at him. "I don't know."

"You don't know?"

"It just seems so . . . sudden."

"Sudden?"

"It seems too fast," she said.

"Too fast? Jess, we've been going out for six months!"

"I know. I just don't know if I'm ready for . . . that."

His face reddened. "What are you scared of?" he said.

"I'm not—"

"You can't be careful all the time, okay? Sometimes you have to take a risk. Sometimes you have to give up being so careful all the time. Come on, Jessica. Take a risk. Do something risky for a change."

Her eyes flashed. "You want risky? You think I'm too careful? I don't see you going to Mali with the youth group. I don't see you doing anything like that."

He rolled his eyes. "Okay."

"Okay? Okay, what?"

"Okay, I'll go."

"What?"

"I'll go on the mission trip. It'll be fun. What do I have to do?"

Jessica felt her mouth hanging open, her heart beating wildly. This wasn't what she had in mind. Moments ago she was planning to end her relationship with Shawn. Now he was going to Africa with her?

"I—I don't know," she stammered. "I don't know if you can. It's probably too late."

"I'll find out. Who do I call? Duane Cunningham?"

Her mouth opened and closed several times. She had no idea what to do. "I guess," she said.

He nodded and smiled as though pleased with himself. "Cool. I'll call Duane."

She felt paralyzed. Helpless. Speechless.

He stepped closer to her, took her shoulders in his hands, and kissed her lightly. "This'll be great," he said. "Just promise me you'll think about what I said. Okay?"

She took a deep breath, and exhaled slowly. She nodded. "Okay," she said. "Sure."

Shawn kissed her again then turned and left, shutting the door behind him. She stood in the center of the living room, alone.

✝✝✝✝✝✝✝

"RATSBANE, THAT brilliant brimstone brain of yours has done it again," muttered the ant-headed toad demon to himself. "That Jessica kid is swallowing my Project TruthTwister lies like they were M&Ms. 'What does the Bible mean *to you?*' Ha! She thinks she can make her own truth using the Bible for help if she just tries hard enough. She's responding perfectly. Project TruthTwister is headed for brilliant success. And that Shawn kid . . . he's almost doing my work for me. Once he gets that girl back in his clutches, her virtue will be history. It's almost too easy. And it couldn't be happening at a better time. Things are going so well that I'll have no qualms about leaving my post for a little well-deserved outing tonight."

Ratsbane left the rank-smelling pit, climbed into his two-wheeled rickshaw-like contraption, and reclined in the seat covered with the soft hide of baby kangaroos. He placed each of his scrawny, frog-skinned arms on an armrest fashioned from the thighbone of some large creature and propped up his gangly frog legs on a footrest formed from the skull of an Asian elephant. In Ratsbane's opinion, the vehicle was the most hideously beautiful thing he'd ever seen.

"Grab the handles; let's go." He croaked several orders to Nefarius, who lumbered into position between the long pole-handles and lifted them in his furry hands.

"Move it, you mangy monkey! We're going to be late," Ratsbane complained.

Nefarius started forward, his short legs and long arms combining to create a lumbering motion that pitched his passenger back and forth in the seat like a rag doll in a rocking chair.

"Faster!" Ratsbane said. "The solemn convocation is supposed to start any time now! If you hadn't taken so long to get here, I'd be seated on the stage already. As it is, we'll be lucky to get there before the whole thing ends!"

Nefarius said nothing, but he snarled softly and turned the next corner more sharply than he had to, slamming the rickshaw against the rocky cavern walls and sending Ratsbane off the kangaroo-hide seat and onto the floor of his chariot.

"You stupid sack of sewage! Watch where you're going!" Ratsbane crawled back onto the seat, cursing his assistant with every move.

Finally, the duo entered the massive central cavern of hell where the day's ceremony was to be held. Nefarius stopped, dropped the handles of the rickshaw, and gazed in amazement at the scene.

The vast underground cavern crawled with thousands—maybe millions—of demons of every shape and size. There were demons with scales and others with feathers or fur. Some slithered across the stone floor, and some clung to the viscous walls. Whole sections of the room seemed to writhe with worm-shaped creatures. Many walked on four legs, some on eight, others on two. Their red eyes glowed in the gloomy expanse of that room, multiplying the impact of their great number.

"Take me to the stage!" Ratsbane ordered, but Nefarius seemed not to hear him above the cacophony of the room; barks, growls, caws, howls, roars, cackles, screams created a babel of confusion and disharmony. "I said, take me to the—"

Ratsbane threw his hands up in frustration and leaped out of the rickshaw. His long legs vaulted him in one move onto Nefarius's furry back. He grabbed the thick matte of hair on his assistant's shoulders and pressed his bulbous ant head against Nefarius's walrus head.

"To . . . the . . . stage," he ordered. "Now!" He gripped a handful of his assistant's chin whiskers in his fingers and yanked them out.

Nefarius bawled and shook himself violently, but Ratsbane held on.

"To the stage!" he repeated.

With a lunge, Nefarius bounded into the crowd with Ratsbane riding on his back like a cowboy. The ape-walrus barreled across the room, shoving his fellow demons to one side then the other as he literally threw his weight into the task. He seemed to take a perverse pleasure (the only kind of pleasure demons ever experience) in hurting as many members of the massive audience as possible, though Ratsbane noticed that he generally avoided attacking demons that had tusks, claws, or fangs.

After a long orgy of inflicting pain on one demon after another, Nefarius finally reached the stone stage at the center of the enormous cavern. Ratsbane sprang from his assistant's back and onto the stage, landing with a satisfied croak.

"Stay right there," he croaked at Nefarius. "Be ready to lead me out of this room in majesty and splendor when the ceremony is over." With great effort, he stood as straight as possible on his gangly legs and lifted his gigantic head to gaze around him. Other than those whom Nefarius had thrown out of their path, the raucous crowd had not noticed his ascent to the stage. The entire throng continued to bicker and bite, scowl and scream, like angry humans in a traffic jam.

A shadow suddenly descended into the already-darkened cave. Many in the great mass of demons cowered, as though expecting an attack from above. Others lifted their gaze toward the high ceiling. The room quieted.

A mysterious form floated about the room, spreading darkness everywhere it flew. It circled silently, malevolently, until the room was as silent as a tomb. Then it swooped and landed majestically at the center of the stage.

The form belonged to a demon with the body and neck of a huge heron, a water bird with long legs and broad wings, and the enormous head of a snake.

"Mallus!" Ratsbane whispered. He gazed in wonder at his former superior from Subsector 1122. They had worked together on the Prime-Evil Impulse Transducer, but when Mallus was crushed beneath a piece of equipment during a particularly powerful backdraft, Ratsbane, as the highest-ranking survivor, had taken Mallus's position.

"Sssurprisssed to sssee me?" Mallus spoke in a clear voice with a faint hissing sound that seemed to come from somewhere behind the his words. His serpent tongue darted in and out of his mouth as he spoke, giving the impression that Ratsbane was about to become his next meal.

Ratsbane nodded. "I—I . . . Yes, Your Malevolence."

Mallus's head turned slowly as he gazed at Ratsbane, first with one slitted eye, then with the other. "I lossst my head," he said.

Ratsbane hesitated, expecting the mighty snake-bird to say more. It seemed as if everyone in the cavernous room was watching, though even the demons closest to them could probably hear little. "Well, m-mighty Mallus," Ratsbane stammered, "we all lose our heads once in a while."

In a flash, Mallus cuffed Ratsbane with a mighty swipe of his wing. Ratsbane staggered back a step, but he managed to maintain his footing as a low rumble of hungry grunts and smacking lips coursed through the crowd.

"I meant it literally," Mallus hissed. "I lossst my head from the backdraft in Ssubssector 1122. I don't exsspect you to notissse the differenssse. But thissss," he said, nodding his viper head, "iss a cottonmouth, the deadliessst of sssnakess. Quite an improvement, don't you think?"

Ratsbane worked his mandibles, inwardly cursing his inability to affect an ingratiating smile. "Oh, yes, Your Maliciousness. It is a truly hideous improvement, yes, absolutely."

Mallus spread his wings, prompting Ratsbane to duck in anticipation of yet another blow. The imposing snake-bird only turned to survey the crowd.

"Demonssss!" he hissed, his voice suddenly and astoundingly filling the room. "Evil rulerss and authoritiesss of the unsseen world, mighty powerss of darknessss, wicked spiritsss, we gather in this convocation to presssent the greatessst and foulessst award in hell—the Ignoble Prize!"

A frightening, deafening roar arose from the crowd as they all united, not to honor the recipient, but to grovel and fawn over the mighty Mallus, hoping his serpent eye might take notice and perhaps elevate them to a higher station in hell.

"The resssipient," Mallus continued, "receivesss the Ignoble Prize for hisss work on Project TruthTwissster, in which he isssolated a few key missconceptionsss that have transssformed the effectivenesss of our demonic effortss in a multitude of human beingsss, ssimultaneous-sly breaking the heart of our Enemy himssself!"

A chorus of cruel and gruesome cries exploded from the dark assembly, washing over Ratsbane like a cool ocean wave. When the crowd quieted, a buzzard flew into the room, descended to the stage, set a glittering statuette at Ratsbane's webbed feet, then quickly flew off again.

"My sssinissster ssspiritss, I give you the Ignoble Award winner, the Detessstable Ratsssbane!"

Ratsbane stretched himself to his full height. The room erupted in a deafening bedlam of hateful cries, jeers, and insults as every demon expressed his insane jealousy and resentment of the award winner. Ratsbane received the denunciations with the closest thing to happiness he'd ever experienced, occasionally even feeling the thrill of being spit on by his fellow demons. He stooped to pick up the dazzling statuette, which resembled an angel of light, and held it aloft for his envious peers to see. To no one's surprise, it slowly changed shape, morphing into a mass of worms and maggots in Ratsbane's hands.

† † † † † † †

JESSICA SAT on her bed and balanced her laptop computer on her knees. Her online journal was open on her screen. She fingered the tiny teardrop pendant around her neck with one hand as she used the other hand to scroll through the last several entries she had written. She read some of the encouraging responses a couple members of the youth group had entered. It was so much easier to spill her thoughts and feelings onto the screen than to trust her feelings to someone face-to-face. It seemed weird, but she didn't think she could ever talk to Sarah and Alison and Anna about the things she wrote in her online journal.

She let her pendant drop and placed both hands on the keyboard.

> i can't seem to stop messing things up. i know I'm doing all the right things. i read my Bible and pray. i've even been memorizing some verses, so that's all good, right? and i love God, i really do, and i know he loves me. so why do i feel like nothing's working? the youth group's really great. i'm glad i'm a part of it. but here i am again just like every other night ready to go to bed (my mom's been asleep for an hour, i bet. she works so hard. i worry about her all the time) and i don't know, i feel so . . . empty. why do i feel that way when i'm doing all the things a christian is supposed to do?

She stopped typing. The online journal included a messaging function, so sometimes when she was typing her journal entry one of her friends, like Sarah, Pastor Milford's daughter, would message her and they would talk online even while she added to her journal. But the messaging screen showed no activity, so she continued typing.

> i guess i'm just in a bad mood because i've been looking forward to the mission trip to Mali for so long, thinking it's gonna be a chance to like, get away from everything and maybe find something, like maybe do something really cool for God, something that would really make a difference. it might help make God ease up on me for the way shawn and my relationship has been going. but i feel like i sorta messed up there, too.

She stopped. She hadn't given Shawn the password to her journal yet, but she still didn't want to say too much. She hadn't written about the guilt she'd been feeling because she and Shawn had gone too far a couple times. She hadn't journaled her thoughts about breaking up with Shawn. And she probably never would.

i just hope i don't ruin the trip. for me or for anyone. i was really wanting to get away and maybe think clear for once. maybe finally have the time to look deep inside myself and work out some way to get to where i could feel like God isn't disappointed in me.

She stared at the words on the screen for a few moments. Every single time she made an entry in the online journal she wrestled with the temptation to delete it. A couple times she had given in to the temptation. But tonight she would keep it. She stared for a long moment then typed in two more words:

we'll see.

She pressed the "Enter" key and posted her thoughts into her journal. That done, she lingered, drawing invisible circles on the computer screen with her cursor arrow. She wished some of her youth group friends would come online. She longed for someone to message her . . . someone . . . anyone. But there was no one to make her feel less alone, less empty, so she shut down the computer, folded up the screen, and placed it on the floor beside her bed.

† † † † † † †

(THE INSIDE STORY)
SO FULL OF EMPTINESS

Jessica feels alone . . . but she's not. Not really.

She became a Christian not long ago, thanks to the influence of Sarah Milford in her life. She felt so happy when she allowed the forgiveness of God to flood her soul. She would tell you that she remembers "feeling warm all over." In that moment, she felt so grateful for God's gift of salvation and deliverance from the weight of her sins. It was an experience she wouldn't trade for anything in the world, and one she'll never forget. All the elation Jessica felt at that moment was well justified, for when she gave her life to Christ, God's Holy Spirit entered her life. He took up residence in her soul and became available to her as the power she could depend on to transform her life into one of Godlike living. I don't mean a power like a Star Wars force, available for anyone to use for his or her own purposes, right or wrong. The Holy Spirit is not a disembodied force that we can plug into. He is a real person, alive and loving, who comes literally into our lives and enables us to be what God wants us to be. He's not a power we control, but a person we submit to.

Jessica's experience of salvation was just the beginning, and the road since that moment has been more than a little bumpy. While she has never been truly alone since the Holy Spirit came into her life, she has not always relied on him for guidance, for a relationship to fill her emptiness, or for transformation in her life. In fact, she sometimes forgets he's even there and tries to improve her life by her own power. That's why when her road gets bumpy, she gets easily confused, empty, lonely, and despondent.

If you have experienced salvation in Jesus Christ (particularly if it happened recently), you probably remember what happened when you confessed your sins, asked God's forgiveness, and invited Jesus into your heart to control and guide your life and help you obey him from that moment on. Your sins were forgiven (Ephesians 1:7). You received a new start, a totally new life in Christ (2 Corinthians 5:17). You were given the Holy Spirit to live inside you. He not only made you feel new and clean inside, but he also brought with him the love, peace, and joy that are the fruit of having the Spirit in you.

It felt like a whole new beginning, didn't it? But it was only that: the beginning. You were probably aware that there would still be times of discouragement and frustration. You probably didn't think everything would be just "happy happy joy joy" all the time.

If you're anything like Jessica, however, you didn't think you would still struggle with strong feelings of loneliness and emptiness. You didn't think you'd keep "messing things up." You might have thought, like her, that as long as you did all the right things (like reading your Bible and praying every day—maybe even going so far as to memorize a few Bible verses), everything would pretty much work out, right?

Would it surprise you to learn that a lot of Christian kids—like Jessica—feel like nothing's working? They may not even realize it, much less talk to someone about it, but deep down they feel empty. Unfulfilled. Alone. Like something's missing.

Some try to deny their feelings or simply "tough it out." Some resign themselves to feeling that way. Others convince themselves that their excitement at finding new life in Christ and experiencing God was a fluke or a passing mood.

Some, like Jessica, try harder to do all the "right" things, even going on a mission trip or doing something similarly courageous or selfless to try to "get back" what they feel is missing. They may see it as building up credit with God, so perhaps he'll back off from punishing them too severely when they do wrong.

Some, like Shawn, try to fill their emptiness any way they can: concerts, activities, parties, friends, girlfriends, and sometimes the thrill of deliberate danger. Yet even when those pursuits are harmless, even healthy, they do little to fill the emptiness inside.

Jessica and Shawn know they are each missing something. The problem is that their enemies, the denizens of hell, also know it. The demons know what is missing and what will fill that emptiness and ease the sense that "nothing's working." And they will do everything they can to prevent Jessica and Shawn—and you and me—from discovering it.

CHAPTER THREE

Shawn followed Jessica through the door, expecting to escape the stuffy swelter of the plane. But exiting the plane at the airport in Bamako, Mali's capital city, felt like walking through the open door of a furnace.

"What a beautiful day!" Jason said, stepping out of the plane just behind Shawn.

"Yeah," Shawn said, "if you like sweating like a . . . like a . . ."

"Like a dinosaur in a meteor shower?" Jason offered. "Like a ditchdigger in a rock quarry? Like a lobster in a seafood restaurant?"

Each member of the Westcastle mission team had been instructed to wait on the tarmac for the others upon landing, so Shawn and Jessica slowed as they reached the bottom of the stairs that had been rolled to the door of the plane. Even before they stepped aside, however, men and women jostled past them, many of them carrying empty plastic water bottles and rumpled napkins they had gathered before exiting the plane.

"We're here," Shawn said.

Jessica nodded without smiling.

"Are you okay?" he asked.

She nodded again. "Yeah, sure."

"I can't believe it. I never thought I'd make it. I mean, everything happened so fast, you know?"

Yeah, Jessica thought. *I know.*

"I hope Jonah's okay." Shawn had been able to join the mission team less than a week before departure only because Jonah Madison had contracted a nasty infection, preventing him from making the trip.

Moments later, the ten-member mission team stood together on the dark tarmac. Duane and Liz Cunningham, the youth leaders of Westcastle Community Church, performed a quick visual check of the group and led the way toward the terminal. Jessica and Shawn, along with Sarah Milford, Ryan Ortiz, Alison Cheney, and D.J. Chen followed, with Darcelle Davis and Jason Withers bringing up the rear.

✝✝✝✝✝✝✝

(THE INSIDE STORY)
JOIN THE CROWD

If you've read any of the previous novels in the Powerlink Chronicles series, you've already met some of the characters in this book. Even if you've followed the Westcastle youth group since their first appearance in *Under Siege*, you've already noticed that there are some new faces in the group. Let's take some time now to introduce this courageous group that is about to enter a new culture . . . and a new adventure.

JESSICA FURMAN. Jessica's parents divorced when she was seven; she's now sixteen, and a junior and cheerleader at Eisenhower High School in Westcastle. Sarah Milford, who led Jessica to Christ, has since become her most trusted friend.

SHAWN LEE. Shawn will be a senior when school resumes in the fall at Eisenhower (or "Ike" as nearly everyone calls it). He lives with both his parents, though he doesn't enjoy a close relationship with either. He became part of the Westcastle youth group through his relationship with Jessica.

SARAH MILFORD. The seventeen-year-old daughter of James Milford, the pastor of Westcastle Community Church. Sarah has always known she was adopted and that her birth mother had died when Sarah was two years old. Just last year, she met her biological grandfather, an encounter that changed her life (*The Deceivers,* Tyndale House Publishers).

RYAN ORTIZ. Eighteen-year-old Ryan has just graduated from Eisenhower High and will be attending M.I.T. in the fall on a scholarship. He committed his life to Christ on last year's SWAT (Summit Wilderness Adventure Training) trip with a few members of the Westcastle youth group (*The Deceivers,* Tyndale House Publishers).

JASON WITHERS. Since graduating from Eisenhower High, Jason (who has appeared in every Powerlink Chronicle) has been attending Westcastle Community College and has become a key leader in the Westcastle youth group (without losing his sometimes bizarre sense of humor). He plans to become a youth pastor some day.

DARCELLE DAVIS. Darcelle has also stuck around Westcastle after high school, feeling called to minister in the church and with the youth group. She became a Christian at a summer conference before her freshman year in high school and exerts a quiet but strong leadership everywhere she goes.

ALISON CHENEY. Sixteen-year-old Alison is a good listener, a good talker, and a good sport. Her father is an alcoholic, and Alison spends as little time at home as she can. While she and Sarah Milford have been good friends since eighth grade, she's still getting to know Jessica and Shawn.

D.J. CHEN. All the girls seem to love D.J., but he hardly notices. His family moved to Westcastle two years ago, and he's been a part of the youth group ever since. He's a track star, a member of the soccer team, and a member of the National Honor Society. He helps his parents run the family restaurant.

DUANE AND LIZ CUNNINGHAM. Duane and Liz, both in their early thirties, recently left their jobs (he as a carpenter, she as a sales clerk) to become full-time youth pastors at Westcastle Community Church. Appearing in all five of the Powerlink Chronicles to date, they've had a huge impact on the lives of many students.

These are not the only people you'll meet in this book, but they're the members of the Westcastle youth group who have made the trip to Mali. It is no coincidence that they also are the main targets of Ratsbane's new, award-winning strategy—a strategy that also targets you and your friends, as we will see.

†††††††

Once inside the terminal building of the Bamako airport, the group stopped behind Duane and Liz. All ten stared in amazement at their shockingly crowded, chaotic, and cacophonous surroundings. The first impression was of widespread panic. People seemed to be moving in every direction, shouting, jostling, and jockeying for position.

Shawn's eyes opened wide at the scene. It was intimidating and frightening but also exciting. He turned to say something to Jason Withers, but Duane spoke above the din before Shawn could say anything.

"Follow us!" Duane shouted. Signs and arrows in multiple languages pointed here and there, but he seemed to ignore them, moving toward two parallel checkpoints where people pressed forward not in lines but in milling mobs heading the same direction.

The group managed some sort of a line and waited for their turn at the customs window.

"Remember, we're going to Mali to accomplish three things." Duane had instructed the group the night before their departure from Westcastle. "First, we are going to West Africa to distribute God's written Word; that's why every member of the group has been issued three Bibles in three different

languages. Many different languages are spoken in Mali, and we will be exposed to people who speak Arabic, Bambara, and Dogon, a tribal language. One of your tasks is to leave each of your Bibles behind by the end of the trip. We've already started praying that God will get those Bibles into the hands of people who will read them and receive the Word of God.

"We're also going," he continued, "to rebuild a mud school among the Dogon people in a village called Ende. There we'll be in a situation where we'll have to be very careful. We're there to build the school, and we've been told that the leaders of the village have agreed to host us, but there is a strong resistance to the gospel of Jesus, so we'll be primarily building friendships and leaving Bibles behind where they'll do the most good. We're going to have to be very courteous and subtle.

"And finally, we're also going to study and pray together in an effort to deepen our own faith by encountering the reliability of God's Word and seeking to experience it in new and fresh ways."

"Several of you have traveled with us before," Liz added, "and you all know how important it is to follow 'the rules of the road,' as your Mission Trip Manual said. I just want to emphasize that every trip has an element of danger to it, so it's important that everyone cooperates fully. We're going to be in a foreign culture, far from home, and while there's no reason to be afraid, we can't afford to have anyone forget 'the rules of the road.'"

"Shawn," said Jason, who with Darcelle had functioned as a leader in the group since graduating from high school several years earlier, "you have an added challenge, since you were only here for the final training session."

Shawn nodded. "I know. I've read the Mission Trip Manual twice already."

Jason smiled. "That's great. I'll give you the exam on the plane."

"Exam?" Shawn asked.

"Exam?" Alison Cheney echoed. "You guys took an exam? Nobody told me!"

Darcelle shook her head and swatted Jason on the back of his head. "He's just playing, girl. There's no exam."

"Are you okay?" Sarah asked Jessica as they inched toward the customs window.

Jessica glanced back immediately at Shawn, but he seemed preoccupied with a woman who balanced a small bag on her head while carrying a child in a cloth sling around her shoulder. She turned back to Sarah. "Yeah, sure," she said.

"You don't seem like it," Sarah insisted. "Something's bothering you, isn't it?"

Jessica flashed a weak smile. "No. I'm okay. Really." She glanced ahead at the long, noisy line of people between the Westcastle group and the customs window. She turned and met Sarah's gaze. Sarah wasn't cutting her any slack. She said nothing, but it was clear that she was waiting for Jessica to say more. Jessica shrugged. "I can't talk now," she said, hoping Sarah would drop it, at least for now.

Jessica finally reached the customs officer after Sarah had been waved through. The surly man in the brown shirt glanced briefly at Jessica's passport and, as he had done with Sarah, impatiently waved her through the checkpoint.

The group regathered at the baggage claim where a loud and boisterous mob of Malian men approached them repeatedly, offering to help. Duane and Liz hovered over the group like mother hens, politely shaking their heads and saying, "Non, merci," at the would-be porters.

"I love Americans!" said a Malian man to Jessica, smiling broadly. "I want to marry American woman. Are you married?"

Jessica smiled back. "No sir," she said.

Suddenly Shawn stepped between Jessica and the man. "She's taken," he said gruffly. He put his arm around her shoulders. "She's mine."

The man shrugged and, smiling, walked slowly away. Jessica whirled to face Shawn.

"I'm *yours*?" she said, her cheeks filling with color. "Is that what you think?"

"Wha—?"

"I belong to you now, huh?"

"I didn't mean—"

She stared at him as though her gaze needed only a magnifying glass to burn a tiny hole in his forehead.

"I just wanted to protect you, okay?" he said. "I didn't mean anything by it."

She tossed her hair and turned to face the rest of the group, whose members suddenly seemed intensely interested in every piece of luggage around them.

Moments later, Shawn grunted as he lifted a heavy suitcase onto a rickety wooden cart. "You okay?" Jason asked.

Shawn blinked. "Oh yeah," he answered. "That wasn't that heavy."

Jason smiled and slapped Shawn on the back of his head. "I wasn't talking about the suitcase. I meant, you and Jessica."

"Oh," Shawn answered, his expression immediately falling. "I don't know."

"I had a girlfriend, once," Jason said.

"Yeah?" Shawn said, anticipating Jason's advice.

"That's it. I had a girlfriend once." Jason shrugged then smiled broadly. "Life's been pretty easy since then."

Shawn smiled weakly. "Yeah, I bet."

"I don't get you two."

"Me neither."

"I mean," said Jason, "you are going out, right?'

"Yeah. At least, I thought so. But she's been funny lately."

"Funny?"

"Yeah. I don't know. Like she's losing interest or something."

"Have you talked to her about it?"

"Well, yeah, sort of," Shawn answered. He told Jason about his conversation with Jessica after Bible study and how her suggestion had led to him coming on this trip. "I've just been so confused ever since then. It's like the closer we get, the weirder it feels."

"That almost sounds like a commercial—for what, I don't know."

"And then you saw what happened today. She's been acting funny the whole trip so far. I think I have to do something to . . ."

"To what?" Jason asked.

"I don't know. Something."

A smirk appeared on Jason's face. "Wow, dude, you're a genius!"

"I am?"

"Yeah. Who else would think of doing . . . . something?"

Shawn cocked his head to one side and examined Jason's smiling expression. Then he got Jason's sarcasm and smiled back.

"All right, crew," Duane announced. "The luggage is all present and accounted for."

"That's amazing!" Darcelle said.

"It really is," Liz agreed. "We always seem to lose something or at least have to wait around a long time for it."

"Well, not this time," Duane said. He turned and draped an arm around a Malian man with dark skin and dark hair, except for a lock of white hair descending from each temple. "I want you all to meet Joe," he said. "Joe is going to be our guide and host for the next week. He will take us to our lodgings in Bamako tonight and help us find our way to the village of Ende."

"Hi Joe," said several members of the group.

"Joe is going to take our luggage to our lodgings for tonight," Duane said, "and then come back to get us."

"I hope we can eat while we wait," Alison confided to Sarah and Jessica. "I'm hungry."

"You're always hungry," Jessica whispered back.

"No, it's not time to eat yet," answered Liz, apparently causing Alison to blush. "It is time for your first assignment of the trip, though."

"That's right, dudes and dudettes," Jason announced.

"Does everyone carry their Arabic Bibles on their persons?"

"What?" asked Alison. "What's he talking about?"

"He means, do you have your Arabic Bible with you," explained Jessica.

"Oh," Alison said. "Why didn't he just say that?"

Jason waited for a response. It took a few moments for all of them except Sarah Milford to indicate that they had their Arabic Bibles. "Sarah?" Jason asked.

Sarah grimaced. "I think it's in my suitcase."

Darcelle clucked her tongue good-naturedly. "Girl," she said, "you'd forget your head if it wasn't attached, wouldn't you?"

"My mom says that all the time," Sarah said.

"Here," Darcelle offered. She extended a Bible in her direction. "I've got an extra." Sarah took it gratefully.

"Now remember," Duane reminded the group. "You're to stay in groups. No one goes anywhere alone. We're in a foreign culture, and you want to leave your Bible where it stands a good chance of finding a new home in someone else's possession. You have to be subtle and not take any chances. You're simply going to set down your Arabic Bible somewhere and leave it behind for someone else to pick up. Is that clear?"

Several in the group nodded, and then they all dispersed.

Jessica and Sarah watched Alison and Darcelle head off into the airport terminal together. "Let's see what they do," Jessica suggested.

They followed and watched as Darcelle and Alison shouldered their way through the crowd.

"Can I ask you something?" Jessica said to Sarah.

"Yeah," Sarah answered, without taking her eyes off Darcelle and Alison.

"What do you think about me and Shawn?"

Sarah glanced at her friend. She wrinkled her brow. "You and Shawn?"

Jessica nodded.

"You mean, as a couple?"

Jessica nodded again.

Sarah watched Darcelle and Alison pause beside a group of people who sang and clapped their hands, smiling and laughing together. "I don't know. I think you guys are cute."

"Do you think we belong together?" Jessica asked.

Sarah hesitated. "You don't?"

Jessica shrugged. They saw Darcelle elbow Alison and nod toward a mother and baby begging by the exit. Side by side the girls approached the woman. Darcelle crouched beside her, setting the Bible down on the terminal's concrete floor as she opened a tiny purse and searched through it. She pulled out some coins and pressed them into the woman's hand with a smile. The mother nodded and spoke rapid words that Darcelle couldn't understand. Nodding back, Darcelle stood, leaving the Bible on the ground at the woman's side. She and Alison walked away, triumphant smiles on their faces.

"That was cool," Sarah said.

"Yeah," Jessica agreed. "Darcelle makes everything look easy."

✝✝✝✝✝✝✝

RATSBANE, WAS in an exceptionally good mood, still basking in the glory of the Ignoble Prize ceremony. Despite the disintegration of the statuette, he reminded himself that every demon in that sector of hell had seen it in his hands. The only thing that could have made the moment better was if he'd had the opportunity to rub every demon's nose in it.

He let out an involuntary croak of pleasure and looked up from the intelligence report he'd just received from HAVOC, hell's super-secret spy agency. He sat behind a desk of immense proportions in a cavern that, while still dank and slimy, befit his position as the newest Ignoble Prize winner and the genius of Project TruthTwister.

"Nefarius!" he bellowed. "Get in here! And make it quick!"

A foul smell filled the room, followed by the apish form of Ratsbane's assistant.

"Bring up coordinates C46 and L14 on the plasma screen," Ratsbane ordered.

Nefarius grunted and reached for the controller which lay on Ratsbane's massive desk, right beside the over-demon's froggish elbow. Ratsbane loved to give orders, and he particularly loved to watch his subordinates do tasks he could do for himself.

Nefarius pointed the controller at the large screen on the wall across from Ratsbane's desk, and a moment later a high definition image of the Bamako airport filled the screen. Ratsbane scanned the scene for a few moments and saw Darcelle move to the beggar and child.

"Humph!" he grumbled.

Nefarius's eyes widened as he watched the events in the airport. He pointed to the Bible in Darcelle's hands. "Is—is that what I think it is?"

Ratsbane's eyes narrowed. "Yes, you bulging bladder of rancid lamp oil; that is a Bible. You dolt! It's not like you've never seen one before."

"Can't you do something?!" Nefarius pleaded.

"Oh, grow up, you mound of manure."

"But—but look!"

"Yes, I know," Ratsbane answered. "Doesn't that pea brain of yours understand anything about Project TruthTwister? We don't care if these kids have Bibles."

"You—y-y-you don't?" Nefarius stuttered, his walrus eyes wide in shock.

"No!" Ratsbane replied. "Not the way they're using them. As long as they just read the blasted book for what it means *to them,* we can even encourage Bible study. Haven't you read the TruthTwister report?"

Suddenly the thick skin of Nefarius's face flushed with guilt. He shifted his gaze away from Ratsbane's black eyes. "I—I, sure, sort of, I mean, some—"

"You can't even lie convincingly, you slobbering piece of fly bait!" Ratsbane sneered. He gripped the whiskers of Nefarius's bulbous muzzle and pulled until the two demons were head-to-head and eye-to-eye with each other. "It's no wonder you always act ignorant, because you are! Listen to me, you dental disaster, and I'll try to explain it so your pathetic little mind can grasp it. The Bible is no threat to our plans for these humans as long as it's no more than a springboard to subjective believing in their minds."

"Springboard to . . . what?"

Ratsbane's bulbous eye started to rotate wildly in its socket. "Subjective believing! I should have known; you don't even know the meaning of the words. Kids like these have studied the Bible all around the world, and hell is no worse off for it. As long as they continue to create *their own truth* with the 'help' of the Bible, hell's plans can proceed with little difficulty. As long as they view the Bible as a nice little storybook or a source of inspiration for forming their own truth, we've got them right where we want them."

"But—but Bibles are dangerous." Nefarius scratched his bullet head with his hairy paw. "I—I don't get it."

"Of course you don't get it," Ratsbane replied. "It takes a brain to get it. That's why you're now just a low-life bumbling assistant and I'm the Ignoble Prize-winning head of this sector. Let me explain it slowly and simply, and maybe it'll penetrate that blubbery skull of yours. These kids think they're good Christians because they study the Bible once a week. As long as they think the important thing is what it means *to them,* it will never occur to them to dig out the truth about what it *really* means. We'll lead them straight down here to us, and they'll never suspect they're moving."

"I—I see," said the assistant demon, still eye-to-eye with Ratsbane's great ant head.

"Our job is very simple, really, so even a molecule-sized brain like yours should grasp it. We in Project TruthTwister must focus all our energy on just one thing: We must not let those kids see that truth is real and must be discovered, not created."

"Discovered, not created," Nefarius echoed.

"And they must never learn to approach the Bible as the absolute, definitive, reliable Word of you-know-who. They must never let its truth become an objective standard in their lives. Do you hear me?"

"Y-yes," Nefarius answered. "Discovered not created. Never. No. That would be bad. Bad." Ratsbane released the sub-demon's whiskers and the apish body slumped back in the chair.

"But . . . but look!" Nefarius bleated, pointing to the screen. "Those kids are giving Bibles to other people—people whose minds we haven't yet contaminated with Project TruthTwister."

Ratsbane looked up at the screen. Panic seized him. He leaped atop his desk and snatched the controller from his subordinate's paw. He pointed and clicked at the screen. A turkey-headed demon with the body of a cow appeared in an inset box. Realizing he mustn't let Nefarius see him out of control, Ratsbane reined in his panic. "Ah," he said, "as you can see, I've got everything under control. Rankmeat is on site in Mali. Let's see how he handles it."

Ratsbane grabbed a tiny device from one corner of his desk and flipped it open. He held it up for Nefarius to see. "Cell phones," he said. "One of hell's greatest inventions, wouldn't you say?"

Nefarius wiped a string of walrus slobber from his mouth and nodded. "Good thing our operatives dominate the whole industry, too."

Ratsbane peered at the inset on the plasma screen and watched as Rankmeat picked up his own cell phone. "Any idea whether that woman can read?" he asked.

He listened for a moment before responding, "Good, good. Then make sure she keeps that Bible. Don't let her give it away. As for the others, just do what you can to keep those things from being found and read, all right?"

✝✝✝✝✝✝✝

(THE INSIDE STORY)

THE DISCOVERY CHANNEL

Nefarius is not the only one who has trouble grasping hell's strategy. It's, well, nefarious. Cunning. Diabolical.

If you're anything like the vast majority of kids today, you're having trouble understanding what Ratsbane is talking about. You may have been conditioned to believe that your beliefs are very personal and subjective. You may have the opinion that it's up to you to put together a "belief system" that works for you. You might even figure you're supposed to use the Bible as a source for creating a personal truth you can believe in.

Surveys show that most young people (61 percent) believe the Bible provides "a clear and totally accurate description of moral truth," but they don't believe that means the Bible is authoritatively true for everyone.[1] The vast majority of kids your age—81 percent—claims that "all truth is relative to the individual and his/her circumstance."[2]

Having been taught that it's up to them to create their own truth, to decide whatever is true for them, many kids are uncomfortable with any suggestion that a particular viewpoint is true for everyone. So, when they approach

---

[1] Barna Research Group, "Third Millennium Teens" (Ventura, Calif.: The Barna Research Group, Ltd., 1999), 44.

[2] Ibid., 43.

the Bible—if they read or study it at all—they don't see it as a universally true revelation of the one true God. They see it as a mere resource, a set of inspirational stories and helpful insights that might offer guidance in creating their own "truth."

That helps to explain why many good Christian kids adhere to some biblical standards but violate others. Some Christian kids will say that adultery is wrong but premarital sex is okay. Some insist that lying to a friend is wrong but cheating on a test—especially if you had a good reason for not studying—is all right. Many sincerely believe that when they choose to believe something, it becomes true for them simply because they believe it. Thus, they go to the Bible not to discover the truth but to use it as a sort of self-help book for concocting their own version of what's true and false, good and evil, right and wrong.

But Jesus said it is possible to know the truth—objectively, apart from your own opinions and feelings. He said, "You will know the truth, and the truth will set you free" (John 8:32). He prayed to his Father, "Teach them your word, which is truth" (John 17:17). He didn't say, "Your word is a springboard to truth," or "Your word will help them find the truth." He didn't even say, "Your word will equip them to find what's true for them." He said, "Your word is truth," objectively. The Bible is the means by which the one true God has chosen to reveal details of himself to you and me. When you hold a Bible in your hand, you are cradling a holy book to be reverenced and hungered after because its very words reveal the God who gives your life its true purpose.

But, of course, if the truth isn't something we're supposed to create for ourselves—if it is something we must discover—then the next question is only fair to ask: "Is the Bible a reliable source for discovering truth?"

CHAPTER FOUR

Jason stopped. "Eleven o'clock," he said.

Shawn glanced at him in puzzlement. He looked at his watch. "No, it's not."

Jason nodded ahead of them and slightly to the left. "Not eleven o'clock, chronologically; *eleven o'clock* geometrically."

Shawn looked in the direction Jason had indicated and saw a man beside an obviously homemade cart filled with something that looked like fruits and nuts. Jason strode in the man's direction, digging in his pocket for change. Shawn understood; Jason was going to buy something from the man and leave the Bible on his cart after making his purchase.

Not to be outdone, he looked all around and saw, just a few feet away, a sleeping man, bearded, draped in a bright blue robe with a veil covering much of his head. Shawn quickly glanced around and saw that Jason was nodding at the vendor and holding something in his hand, apparently finishing their transaction.

Shawn leaned over, hesitating only a moment, and gingerly set his Arabic Bible on the man's blue-robed lap. He slowly backed away without looking behind him.

Shawn felt himself bump into something—something that wasn't there a moment ago. He turned and, horrified, saw an over-laden wooden cart teeter on one wheel. Despite the efforts of the wiry man who held the cart by two wooden handles, the top-heavy vehicle toppled onto its side, sending woven baskets and colored beads bouncing and rolling in every direction. Shawn hardly had time to adjust to the incredible sight when he heard a voice bellowing behind him. He turned to see the blue-robed man waving the Arabic Bible in the air in Shawn's direction and shouting in a strange language.

Surrounded by chaos, Shawn tried to address the shouting man. He then whirled to try to help the vendor pick up the baskets and beads, only to turn again and try hopelessly to mollify the angry man.

"Help him." Jason came up beside Shawn and pointed to the vendor, whose baskets and beads had traveled astounding distances in every direction. Shawn opened his mouth to attempt an explanation, but Jason had already turned away to face the man in the blue robe.

Shawn watched Jason's efforts to pacify the man slowly take effect. The rest of the group—including Jessica—had arrived on the scene. Within moments, they all fanned out to collect wayward baskets and beads, while Duane took over the peacemaking task from Jason.

Shawn watched with embarrassment as Duane gently accepted the Arabic Bible from the man. He passed it to Liz, who nonchalantly dropped it in a basket and added it to the towering stack on the vendor's cart before offering the vendor what looked like a few folded pieces of Malian currency.

"Duane, man, I couldn't feel worse, really," Shawn said. He and Duane led the group out of the oppressive atmosphere of the bustling terminal and into the sweltering sun of the Malian day.

Duane shook his head without irritation. "Don't sweat it," he said. "We'll just learn from it and move on."

The group met up with Joe, their guide and interpreter, who opened the doors of a dingy white van and waved them inside.

"Hang on, everybody," Liz shouted as Joe pulled the van into traffic. "Traffic here can be pretty crazy." Every window in the van was open, and the noise of the traffic swirled around them while the knocking of the van's engine seemed to beat a drum tempo on their brains.

Duane swiveled in the front seat to face the group. "We're staying in Bamako tonight," he said. "It'll take us about an hour to get there. I want to remind everyone that we're in a foreign culture, and we need to be really careful."

Shawn caught Duane's eye.

"It's okay, Shawn," Duane said. "I'm not blaming you for what happened back there. I just want to make sure everyone knows we're going to have to be as polite and subtle as possible while we're here. Things don't operate the same way they do back home—especially when it comes to sharing God's Word. In fact, we'll be experiencing several cultures, not just one, and each one is a little different."

"We'll try to talk more about that tonight," Liz added, "when we have devotions together."

Jessica seethed.

"Is something wrong?" Liz whispered to her as they bounced side-by-side, their van jouncing along the pothole-ridden road.

Jessica couldn't bring herself to meet Liz's gaze. She shrugged.

"What is it?" Liz prodded.

"Nothing."

"Come on, Jessica, you know I'm not going to let you get away with that answer. Something's bothering you."

Jessica rolled her eyes but said nothing.

"Okay," Liz conceded. "This isn't the best place to talk." She swept windblown strands of hair out of her face, gathering them together and holding them in place over her right ear as she talked. "Will you tell me later? When we get to where we're staying?"

Jessica finally looked at Liz. She nodded. "Sure, okay," she said. "It's no big deal."

✝✝✝✝✝✝✝

The group arrived at a small church in Bamako. The pastor, who lived in a few rooms at the back of the church with his wife and three children, had welcomed them and served them dinner. After dinner they made sleeping quarters by rearranging the chairs and pews in the church's low-ceilinged sanctuary to divide the room into two sides. The women would sleep on mats and in sleeping bags on one side of the room and the men would sleep on the other side.

As the group began the task of settling into their lodgings for the night, Jessica knelt on the concrete floor of the church and tried to reorganize her suitcase. "How can so much dust get inside a suitcase?" she asked, addressing no one in particular.

Liz's voice answered Jessica's question. "It's amazing, isn't it?" she said.

Jessica turned and clapped a hand to her chest. "You scared me!"

"I'm sorry," Liz said, dropping to one knee beside Jessica and placing a comforting hand on her shoulder. "I didn't mean to sneak up on you."

Jessica patted her chest and sighed. "It's okay. I guess I was just concentrating too hard on all the dust in my clothes. Is everybody's suitcase like this?"

Liz nodded. "I'm afraid so. We'll probably just have to get used to it."

Jessica shook her head, still amazed.

"Is this a good time to talk?" Liz asked.

Jessica turned her gaze back to her suitcase. "Yeah, sure," she said. "I guess there's not much I can do about my clothes."

Liz sat on the floor, leaning against the wall beside Jessica's suitcase. "Something was bothering you when we got into the van."

Jessica cocked her head to one side, thinking. Neither of them spoke for some time. She swung out of her kneeling position, crossed her legs, and faced Liz. "I don't know," she said with a verbal shrug.

Liz waited. Jessica studied the chipped paint on the church walls.

"I guess it's just Shawn," she said.

"Shawn?" Liz asked, as though she hadn't been expecting that answer.

"Yeah. He really messed up, you know?"

"You mean in the airport?"

Jessica bobbed her head as if the answer should be obvious. "Well, yeah. I mean, I don't want to get him in trouble or anything, but I couldn't believe Duane just let him off like he did."

Liz's mouth hung open. "Aren't you and Shawn dating each other?"

Jessica hung her head and played with her shoestring. "Yeah, sort of. But that has nothing to do with this. I just think when somebody messes up . . ."

"You think Shawn meant to cause a scene?"

"No," Jessica said, impatience creeping into her voice. "It's just, well, there has to be some consequence, doesn't there?" She peeked at Liz from under her eyebrows.

Liz blinked as if Jessica's words were a total mystery to her.

"I mean," Jessica continued, "maybe he shouldn't be sent home or anything like that, but I couldn't believe Duane just said, 'Don't sweat it.'"

"So what do you think should be done?" Liz asked.

Jessica sighed. She could tell Liz didn't understand, and that just frustrated her more.

"What do you think God would do?" Liz added.

Jessica's head snapped up and she met Liz's gaze. "Well, that's obvious," she said. "He would have to punish him."

"Punish him?" Liz blurted.

"Yeah."

"Is that really what you think?"

It was Jessica's turn to be shocked. "Don't you? I mean, God can't let people go around getting away with stuff."

"That's the whole reason the Father sent Jesus," Liz said. "To take our punishment. The Bible says that Jesus was pierced for our transgressions and crushed for our iniquities. That means he took our punishment, so we wouldn't have to."

"I know that," Jessica said. "But I'm not talking about that. I'm saying, God still has to punish us when we mess up."

"But Jessica, the Bible says that God's mercies are new every morning. He is loving and gracious and forgiving toward all he has made."

"Yeah, sure," she said. "But to me, that doesn't mean he just, you know, lets people mess up without having to punish them."

"That's exactly what it means. Especially in a case like Shawn's where he didn't sin, he didn't intend to do wrong; God's not waiting to punish him for that."

"I think he is," Jessica insisted.

"How can you say that, when the Bible says different?"

"Because it doesn't mean that to me."

Liz shook her head vigorously. "Jessica, Scripture isn't up for grabs. It's not subject to your own private interpretation. It means what it means."

"Not if it doesn't mean that *to me*."

Liz frowned; she seemed to be struggling to focus her thoughts or form the right words. She stared, holding Jessica's gaze. After a few long moments of hesitation, she again shook her head vigorously, reached over, and took both of Jessica's hands in her hands. "Jessica," she said slowly, as if choosing her words carefully, "I know that sometimes two people can read the same verse or passage of Scripture and each learns something unique or can be touched in a different way . . ."

Jessica nodded, her gaze fastened on Liz's intense eyes.

"But," Liz continued, "are you saying that you think the words of the Bible can have two different *meanings* to two different people?"

Jessica hesitated only a moment before nodding again. "Yeah," she answered. "Isn't that what you're saying?"

Liz shook her head slowly, still holding Jessica's gaze. "No. We're saying two very different things, dear."

Jason Withers's bellowing voice filled the room, imitating the sound of the Bamako Airport P.A. system as he called everyone to assemble for devotions.

"What's this?" Duane Cunningham held a Bible in his right hand and faced the group.

Jessica, like the others in the room, blinked dumbly at Duane, as though the answer to his question was so obvious it wasn't worth mentioning.

"Uh," attempted Ryan. "A Bible?"

Duane smiled. "What else?"

Everyone seemed hesitant. Jessica exchanged glances with Sarah and Alison before answering. "A book?"

"What else?"

Jason spoke slowly, as though pronouncing a great truth. "About a hundred and fifty pieces of acid-free paper between two imitation leather covers."

Duane rolled his eyes in mock disgust. "What else? Anybody."

"The Word of God," said Alison.

"The Old and New Testaments," said Ryan.

"The sword of the Spirit!" answered Darcelle.

"Good," Duane said, before adding, "big deal."

Jessica joined the others in blinking, surprised at Duane's words.

"No, really," Duane continued. "Big deal. So it's the Bible. The Word of God. What's the big deal?"

"What's he talking about?" Alison whispered to Jessica. She looked genuinely offended by Duane's words.

Jessica whispered back. "I think he's making a point," she said.

"Really," Duane repeated. "What's the big deal?"

"Well, dude," Jason offered, "it's the power of God for salvation for everyone who believes."

"Okay," Duane answered with a shrug, still holding the Bible aloft in his right hand. "But you are all Christians, right? What's the big deal . . . for you? I mean, once you know how to be saved, it's pretty much outlived its relevance for you, right?"

"Oh no," Jessica countered, suddenly getting Duane's point. "I don't think so at all. I mean, I don't know what I'd do without my Bible study. It's about the best part of my week because every time we get together, I find the truth I need for that week, truth that's there just for me, even if no one else can see it."

Duane exchanged a quick glance with Liz and then turned slowly back to face Jessica. "Uh huh." He nodded slowly. "But it's just words on a page, right?"

Jessica knew he was baiting them. She opened her mouth to respond when Shawn spoke.

"It can be totally confusing at times," he said. "At least it is to me."

"But it's more than words on a page," Darcelle said. "Isn't that why we're here? Isn't that why we're passing out Bibles in several languages? Otherwise, why wouldn't we just pass out copies of something else?"

"Yeah!" agreed Jason, with a smirk. "Like my research paper investigating why hot dogs are sold in packs of ten, but hot dog buns are sold in packs of eight!"

"I've wondered that, too!" whispered Alison to Jessica.

(THE INSIDE STORY)
MORE THAN MERE WORDS

Jason's right—hot dogs are sold in packs of ten while hot dog buns are sold in packs of eight.

Darcelle is right, too. If the Bible isn't any more than words on a page, then the Westcastle youth group is wasting its time distributing Bibles—to *any*one in *any* language!

The Bible is, as some in the group said, the Word of God and the "sword of the Spirit." As Jason suggested, the message of the Bible is "the power of God for the salvation of everyone who believes" (Romans 1:16, NIV). It is a road map to heaven, a doorway to eternal life.

It is also God's instruction manual for living. The apostle Paul explains, "All Scripture is inspired by God and is useful to teach us what is true and to make us realize what is wrong in our lives. It corrects us when we are wrong and teaches us to do what is right. God uses it to prepare and equip his people to do every good work" (2 Timothy 3:16-17).

Every command, warning, or story in the Bible is intended to show us the right way. When God's Word says, "Follow this way," "Avoid those places," "Abstain from those actions," or "Embrace those thoughts," it is not trying to restrict us or bully us. God always has our best interests at heart, and his Word is intended to protect us and provide for us. As Moses told the nation of Israel,

> You must always obey the LORD's commands and decrees that I am giving you today for your own good . . . I am giving you the choice between a blessing and a curse! You will be blessed if you obey the commands of the LORD your God that I am giving you today. But you will be cursed if you reject the commands of the LORD your God and turn away from him. (Deuteronomy 10:13; 11:26-28)

As big a deal as all that is, there's an even bigger and more fundamental answer to the question of what the Bible is and why it is important. It is more than words on a page, much more: It is a means to a very important end.

The Bible is the means by which God has chosen to introduce and reveal himself to you so that he can enjoy a relationship with you. He uses his Word to bring us into his kingdom through the experience of salvation, not just so we can escape the punishment our sins deserve, but so we can know him and live in relationship with him. As he told the nation of Israel, "I want you to show love, not offer sacrifices. I want you to know me more than I want burnt offerings" (Hosea 6:6).

He saves us so we can know him, and he gives us his Word as the primary means for getting to know him. Moses understood this, of course; he begged God, "If you are pleased with me, teach me your ways so I may know you" (Exodus 33:13, NIV). God's Word—the record of all his ways—is given to us for a very relational purpose: so we may know him and enjoy all the blessings of a relationship with our loving Creator. When we approach the Scriptures in order to know God and have a relationship with him, it not only blesses our lives here and now but also results in eternal life. Jesus prayed to his Father, "And this is the way to have eternal life—to know you, the only true God, and Jesus Christ, the one you sent to earth" (John 17:3).

Remember how ecstatic Jessica was when she first became a Christian? It is because she had received God's Holy Spirit into her life. This is the relationship we're talking about. It's God coming down to you and living within you. Like any relationship, it takes two to make it work. God does his part; he comes to us. Often we fail to keep the relationship active. We ignore his Spirit within us and even forget that he's there. That's why in spite of reading the Bible, in spite of becoming a Christian, the lives of kids like Jessica seem to be off track. She's not drawing on the power of the relationship that God offers to her.

† † † † † † †

RATSBANE HELD his oversized ant head in both hands, his elbows propped on his massive desk. He stared at the plasma screen on the wall and drummed his amphibian-like fingers against his exoskeletal skull as he watched Duane Cunningham conclude a lively session of discussion and interaction among his group.

"That," said Duane, "is ultimately why we are distributing Bibles in several different languages, using whatever techniques we can. It is the primary means human beings have for getting to know God and beginning and continuing a relationship with our loving Creator."

Ratsbane pointed the remote control until a cursor appeared on the screen. Then, using a trackball in the controller, he rotated the image on the screen away from Duane, settling finally on Liz. He tilted his head to one side, enabling him to fully focus his black soulless eye on her.

"She's going to be trouble," he croaked to himself. No one else was in the room. "I never should have put Rankmeat on this job, the worthless turkey jerky."

As Liz rose to take Duane's place, Ratsbane framed her image squarely in the center of the screen. She emphasized to the group the need for cultural sensitivity and caution in sharing their faith and distributing Bibles. Ratsbane widened the screen and saw that Shawn blushed—and Jessica stared at the floor—as Liz spoke. But it was not the current events that agitated Ratsbane.

He had monitored every word of Liz and Jessica's conversation before devotions. Liz's chat with Jessica had taken a nasty turn, from Ratsbane's perspective.

He picked up the cell phone and connected with Rankmeat. He had removed the demon from operating the console and sent him to be onsite with the group in Bamako. He spoke even before his underling had the phone up to the side of his turkey head.

"For future reference," he croaked, "let me explain to you what was happening when that Jessica girl and that Liz woman were talking. Do you remember when W4254—the one named Liz—said something like, 'The Bible means what it means'?"

"Uh huh," the warbling voice on the other end of the line answered, "and then the other one said, 'Not if it doesn't mean that *to me*.'"

"Oh, so you *were* listening, you moron! Well, listen to this: That's exactly the kind of conversation that can do our project the most harm. You let it go on far too long—"

"But I tried! Remember? I threw a lot of stuff at the older one. I gave it everything I had. Even though I didn't get her off track, I did slow it down a little so they couldn't finish before—"

"Stop!" Ratsbane screeched. "Stop your gobbling! That Liz lady got a peek into Project TruthTwister . . . and you let it happen. Our entire strategy depends on these clueless kids abusing the Bible by reading it only to find what it means *to them*. That's how the truth gets twisted, you fowl-brained bovine. You let that dangerous Liz woman expose our little secret. She knows the Bible means what it means and nothing less. If the others grasp what she's saying, Project TruthTwister crashes and burns. And you'll burn along with it because it'll be all your fault. If it happens again," Ratsbane warned, lowering his voice into the most ominous tone possible from his frog throat, "there will be a barbecue grill with your name on it right next to my desk. Got it?"

Ratsbane could hear a warbled gulp on the other end. "Yes, Your Wickedness. I understand. It won't happen again."

"You're right it won't," Ratsbane croaked, "because you're going to end their stay, do you hear me?"

"End it?" Rankmeat asked.

"That's what I said. I want them headed back to where they came from within twenty-four hours."

"How am I supposed to do that?"

Ratsbane pressed the cell phone harder against his bulbous head, as if expecting the pressure to increase the volume. "I don't care how. I just want it done; do you understand? Whatever it takes, you have to turn this whole thing around and get them out of there. I don't care who gets hurt. I don't care if the whole group ends up at the bottom of a ravine. Just get it done!"

"Yes, Your Wicked—"

Ratsbane flipped his cell phone closed and slammed the device down on his desk.

CHAPTER FIVE

The group approached the Malian village of Ende at midday, after a dry, hot, dusty, and interminably bumpy ride in a van with no air conditioning.

"Joe says we're almost there, everyone," Liz announced as the van jounced along the road. At times they had ridden on a paved highway that was as good as Route 122 through Westcastle; but at other times, the road had become a rutted nightmare or a stream bed. Once it even seemed to disappear completely in a dry field of short grass.

Shawn craned his neck like everyone else in the van, trying to locate the village, but all he could see were a few small children running up the road ahead. Soon the children seemed to be on all sides, waving at them and running alongside the van. They pulled into a conglomeration of mud huts. The van rolled to a dusty stop, and the cramped riders piled out of the van.

"Honey, I'm home," joked Jason as he stretched his back and gazed at the scene. The village seemed to spread out in every direction. There were twenty or thirty huts of varying size and no discernible pattern to the arrangement. Children scurried about everywhere, smiling and chattering, clearly excited by the group's arrival.

Immediately the van was totally surrounded by the people of the village who stared openly at the group. The crowd then parted as though obeying some mysterious signal and a tall, thin man appeared. His skin shone as dark as obsidian, and an impressive stone necklace dangled on the bare, smooth skin of his chest. In his right hand he gripped a tall wooden staff topped with a gnarled knot the size of a fist.

He stopped before Duane and Joe and spoke, looking only at Duane.

"This is the headman of this village," Joe explained. "He welcomes you, and thanks you for coming to his village."

The man spoke again.

"He says," Joe interpreted, "he knows that you have traveled a great distance, and he wishes you to eat from his bowl this evening. That means he would like you to share the evening meal with him."

"Please tell him we are honored," Duane said, nodding and smiling at the man.

Joe relayed Duane's words, and the man nodded solemnly, turned, and walked away. Joe turned and spoke quickly to Duane.

"He means for you all to follow him. He will show you where you will be staying."

Duane, Liz, and the rest of the group hurried to keep up with the headman's long strides. He led them through the village, while the men, women, and children trailed along like participants in a parade. He stopped at two huts located near each other but slightly apart from the others.

"These," Joe explained, after a short exchange with the headman, "are your lodgings." At that, the headman turned and stalked away through the crowd of villagers as abruptly as he had appeared.

Duane turned and faced the group. "The men will sleep in this hut, and the women will take that hut."

"Which one has the satellite dish?" Jason asked without cracking a smile.

"They don't have—"Alison started, then stopped, blushing. She looked around the circle of smiling faces, smiling herself. "I know, I know, it's a joke."

Jessica unzipped her suitcase and opened it. "Ugh," she said. "Everything's dusty again!" She lifted out a once-white blouse and shook it in the air over the suitcase, prompting a tiny dust storm in the shadows of the hut. "Sarah," she said, dropping the blouse atop the other dusty clothes, "did your clothes get all dusty again?"

She turned, but Sarah wasn't there. Someone else was. In the doorway stood a young village girl; Jessica immediately judged her age to be about the same as hers, maybe sixteen or seventeen, though the Malian girl was smaller than Jessica.

"Hi," Jessica said.

The girl didn't answer.

"What's your name?"

No answer.

"Yeah," Jessica said, both to herself and to the girl. "You probably don't speak a word of English, do you?"

The girl just stared.

"I'm Jessica," she said, tapping her index finger to her chest. "Jessica," she repeated.

Jessica thought she detected a response, even the hint of a smile in the girl's expression, but still she said nothing. Jessica smiled and shrugged. She started toward the door, in the girl's direction, and stopped. The girl was pointing at Jessica's neck.

Jessica touched her necklace. It had been a gift from her grandmother, along with the matching bracelet. She'd worn it almost every day for ten years.

> *"Jessica, I want to give you something." Grandma Kesler had just entered Jessica's room. She had knocked lightly on the door, but the only answer seven-year-old Jessica gave was a few muffled sobs. Gran sat on the bed at Jessica's feet and heaved her massive purse onto her lap. Jessica kept her legs pulled up against her chest, but she lifted her face from her folded arms atop her knees. She watched as Gran pulled a tiny paper bag out of her purse and turned it*

upside down, emptying the contents into her palm.

"I had to get this fixed," she said softly, "so I could give it to you. The chain was broken." She set her purse on the floor and, turning to face Jessica more directly, lifted a necklace in both hands. The pendant on the necklace was shaped like a teardrop. "I've had it since I was a girl about your age."

Jessica wiped the tears from her cheeks with the palm of one hand and looked at the necklace, then at her grandmother's wrinkled face. She sniffed, blinking the tears back as much as possible.

Gran reached around Jessica's neck and clasped the necklace while Jessica reached back and held her hair out of the way. Then Gran brought her gnarled hands forward and framed Jessica's cheek, holding her head gently in both hands.

"It's a terrible thing when parents get divorced, Jessica. A terrible thing." Jessica saw tears forming in Gran's eyes as she spoke. "No one should have to go through something like this, and especially not a sweet, lovely girl like you. I want you to know," she let go of Jessica's face and lifted the pendant in one hand, "that I'm crying right along with you."

Jessica realized then that Gran still held something in her hand. Gran lifted Jessica's hand and fastened a bracelet with a teardrop matching the necklace around her wrist. She held Jessica's hand tightly and locked gazes with her. "Every time you put on this bracelet or that necklace," she said, "I want you to think of your ol' Gran and how much she loves you. Will you do that?"

Jessica nodded, and then the tears flooded in again. She crumpled into her Gran's arms and cried while Gran rocked her and cried with her.

Jessica suddenly remembered that the Mission Trip Manual had advised them not to take or wear anything they wouldn't mind losing or giving away. She'd forgotten about the necklace. She seldom went anywhere without it. Once, in ninth grade, she thought she had lost it right before a cheerleading tryout and wouldn't stop looking for it even if it meant losing her chance to make the squad with her best friend, Jennifer Brown. She finally found it in the locker room laundry basket and then went out and gave the best cheer performance of her life. She was far happier to have found the necklace than to have made the squad. She'd barely let the necklace out of her sight since, and she wouldn't sell it or give it away for anything in the world.

She looked at the girl's eyes. They were shy and curious at the same time.

"I'm sorry," she told the girl, even as she realized her words wouldn't mean anything. She tried to convey her meaning with her eyes and tone of voice. "It was a gift," she said, shaking her head. "I'm really, really sorry."

The girl walked away, leaving Jessica feeling stingy and mean. She stood there for a few moments then reached her hands behind her neck and removed the necklace. She took the bracelet off, too, and stowed both in the pocket of her suitcase.

Shawn joined the others as they began the task of building the school early the next morning. Duane explained that there was much to be done, and though the site had already been prepared and materials stockpiled, it would still be a miracle if they were able to get the school "under roof," as they called it, by the end of the week.

Jason supplied the comic relief for the group and Duane provided the expertise, having been in construction before becoming a paid youth pastor. Most of the work had to be done in the mornings and evenings since it was too hot to work at midday.

As they worked together, Darcelle started singing one of her favorite worship songs, and Liz soon joined her. Before long, Shawn was singing along with the rest of the group. When one song ended, a few minutes would pass, and someone would start another.

This had been going on for much of the morning when the tall man who had welcomed them the day before approached the group. He looked sternly at them as they worked and then stalked away.

"Wasn't that the head guy of the village?" Shawn asked Jason.

Jason nodded. "Yeah," he said. "He didn't look happy."

Shawn and Jason watched as Joe, the group's Malian guide, approached Duane. The two men stepped aside, and moments later Duane called the group together.

"The chief man of the village," Duane explained, "has asked us not to sing worship songs while we work."

"What?" Ryan asked, adjusting the makeshift sweat-band he wore around his forehead. "You're kidding, right?"

Duane and Joe shook their heads in unison.

"I'm afraid not," Duane answered.

"That's unbelievable!" D.J. said. "Can they even understand what we're singing?"

"Apparently they can recognize one word that we use over and over again," Duane said.

D.J. nodded knowingly. "Jesus," he said.

"That's right," Duane said.

The group looked around at each other for a few moments in stunned silence.

"What do we do?" asked Darcelle.

"It seems so silly," said Jessica.

"Yeah," said Sarah, "but Duane and Liz said there would be strong resistance. We have to be really polite and subtle, right?"

"We came here to serve these people," Duane replied, "and build a school. That's a start."

Shawn elbowed Jason then grabbed a shovel. "You won't get blisters by standing around."

"Just one question," Jason asked Duane. "Can we *hum*?"

"Hum?" Duane echoed.

"Yeah, you know," he said. He hummed a few notes of the song they had just been singing.

Duane smiled broadly and shrugged. "I don't see why not," he said.

† † † † † † †

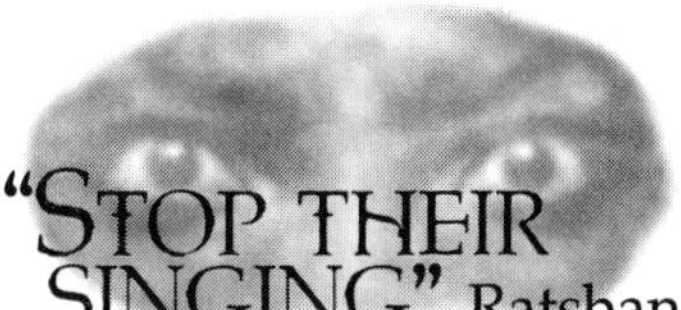

"STOP THEIR SINGING" Ratsbane said. He gazed at the plasma screen, which had just transmitted the encounter between Joe and Duane, and Duane's subsequent conversation with the group. He sighed and turned to Nefarius, who stacked piles of intelligence reports on the corner of Ratsbane's desk. "Is that the best that turkey can do?"

He turned back to the screen and used the trackball on his remote control to rotate the image, taking in the whole scene.

"I don't even see the useless bag of meat," he complained.

Nefarius pointed a furry paw at the screen. "Is that him . . . there?"

Ratsbane pointed the remote at the screen until a cursor appeared. He dragged the cursor to the image Nefarius had pointed out. He pressed a key and the image zoomed in.

It was Rankmeat. He stood on his four cow legs at the edge of the worksite, invisible to the human eyes all around him. Aiming carefully at a pebble on the ground, he positioned himself and kicked at it with one of his hind legs. The pebble skipped across the ground and ricocheted off Jason Withers's forearm.

Rankmeat turned and watched as Jason looked all around him, finally settling his gaze on Shawn who was wrestling a dirt-filled wheelbarrow to the dump site. Jason picked up a pebble and heaved it at Shawn, scoring a hit on his friend's shoulder. By the time Shawn looked around, Jason was humming and working as if nothing had happened.

The turkey-headed cow demon saw Shawn's eyes narrow mischievously before he turned back to his journey with the wheelbarrow. Rankmeat gobbled in delight, then looked for his next victim.

Ratsbane could feel the cold blood in his amphibious body beginning to boil. "Is that the best that incompetent beefy gobbler can do?" he shrieked. He picked up the cell phone, but he was shaking too much to dial. He threw the device at Nefarius. "Call that brainless buffet and tell him he'd better quit playing games or I'll have him over for lunch—and *he'll* be the main course!"

"Yes, Your Putrescence," Nefarius answered as he punched in the numbers.

"Tell him he's going to have to come up with something a lot better than silly complaints about singing, too. I don't care if those kids sing. I don't care if they use the Enemy's name. I don't even care if they have their sweet little disgusting ineffective Bible studies! All I care about is getting that hairy hunk of hay mulch to follow my orders. I told him to get those people out of that country. Ask him if he forgot or does he think he's on some kind of vacation?"

"Sure, boss," said Nefarius. "Let's see now. What's Rankmeat's number?"

"Ohhhh, why do I waste my time!? Give me that phone!" Ratsbane snatched the cell phone from Nefarius's apish paw. "If you want a job done right, you have to do it yourself."

✝✝✝✝✝✝✝

Jessica dropped her work for a moment and grabbed Joe as he turned to walk away.

"Can I ask you a question?" she said. Without waiting for a response, she pointed. The girl who had wanted Jessica's necklace was watching the group from a distance. She walked from one hut to another, hoping to remain unnoticed. "See that girl?"

Joe looked in the direction she was pointing. "Yes," he said.

"Do you know her name?"

"Her name?"

Jessica nodded. "I met her in my hut last night, but I didn't even know how to ask her what her name is."

"You met *her*?"

"Yeah, why?"

Joe's face wore a quizzical look for a moment. Then he shrugged. "It is nothing. Her name is Aya."

"Aya," Jessica repeated.

He nodded. "Aya, yes. She is the chief man's daughter."

Shawn and Ryan joined the others in the group who had gathered for lunch around a large bowl. The heat of the day had become unbearable, and there would be no working for several hours.

"What's that?" D.J. asked. He looked into the bowl.

"It's called *to*," Duane answered, pronouncing the word "toe." "The women of the village have been very kind to prepare this for us."

"Uh huh," D.J. said.

"Come on, D.J.," Jason said. "You're not afraid of a little culinary adventure, are you?"

"Yeah," Ryan joined in. "You and your family eat all kinds of weird stuff at home. What was that thing your mom tried to feed me once? It looked like an old gray egg!"

D.J. smiled. "It's called a hundred-year-old egg."

"Yeah," Ryan remembered. "It looked like somebody rolled it around in soot or something. And it smelled like—"

"Uh, guys?" Liz said. "We're all kind of hungry."

"Oh yeah, sorry," Ryan said, shrugging. "I'm just saying D.J. shouldn't be afraid to eat this stuff; it just looks like mashed-up corn chips."

"That's pretty close," Duane said. The group followed Duane and Liz's lead and gathered around the large bowl in a tight circle. Some squatted while others sat cross-legged. "It's a kind of pudding, I guess you could call it, made from millet."

"What's a millet?" Alison asked.

"A kind of grass," Duane said. "The people here use it a lot, like we use wheat, I guess."

They prayed together, and then, after a simple demonstration from Liz, ate their lunch by taking a round piece of bread (like a pita), dipping it into the bowl, and eating a bite of bread and *to* together.

Shawn had intentionally squeezed into a seat next to Jessica. She had glanced at him when he sat down, but otherwise seemed engrossed in the conversation between Ryan and D.J.

"Hi," Shawn said, as they started eating.

"Hi," Jessica answered.

"I really need to talk to you," he said.

"Yeah," she answered curtly.

"You think we can?"

"Right now?"

"No, not right now. Later. Like . . . today?"

She dipped her bread in the bowl and took a bite. Shawn noticed that she hadn't even looked at him since that quick glance when he sat down. She finished chewing. "Yeah," she said, still not looking at him. "Sure."

He stared at her for a long moment as they ate, his stomach churning. He had eaten all he could.

CHAPTER SIX

Jessica saw Sarah crouched in a corner of the school they were building, mixing something in a bucket. After making sure no one was nearby, she tiptoed over to her friend and tapped her on the shoulder.

Sarah jumped. "You scared me!"

"I'm sorry," Jessica said. "I just need to talk to you."

Sarah patted her chest a few times as if trying to slow her racing heartbeat. She dropped the stick she had been using to stir the mixture in the bucket and sat down in the dirt.

Jessica joined her, sitting cross-legged, facing her friend. "I just don't know what to do," she said.

"About what?" Sarah asked.

"Me and Shawn."

"Oh yeah," Sarah said, remembering their short conversation in Bamako.

"I mean, he's talking like he wants to get more serious."

"And you don't," Sarah said. It wasn't a question.

Jessica shook her head. "I just don't want to break his heart."

"But you've already made the decision."

"I guess I have," Jessica admitted. "Do you think it's the right one?"

"How do I know?" Sarah asked. "Is it just that he wants to get more serious and you don't, or do you not even want to go out—you know, like you've been doing?"

Jessica sighed. She thought of the times she and Shawn had done things she didn't want to do, things she knew didn't please God. "I don't want us to do what we've been doing."

"Do you feel like you have to do something now?" Sarah asked, looking around at their surroundings. "Here?"

Jessica shrugged. "He knows something's wrong. I haven't told him any of this, but he knows things are weird between us. He asked me if we could talk sometime today."

"Then just tell him," Sarah said. "Don't drag it out any longer, but be as kind as you can. At least you know that God would want you to be kind, right? The Bible says we should be kind and tender-hearted to one another."

"Yeah, I know." She stood, and dusted herself off. "Do you need help here?"

Sarah stood and reached for the bucket. "No, I don't think—," but as she picked it up, the bucket tipped to one side; the contents had nearly solidified. She smiled at Jessica. "I guess I need more help than I thought!" she said, and they laughed together.

"This is it," Shawn said. He had seen Jessica walking away from the job site. He wiped his hands on his pants. "Wish me luck."

Jason shook his head. "I'll do better than that, dude. I'll be praying for you."

Shawn jogged in Jessica's direction and caught up with her halfway between the school site and the girls' hut. "Where you going?" he asked breezily, as he fell into step beside her.

She smiled—a sad smile—and answered, "Nowhere."

"Is it okay if we talk now?"

She sighed. "Sure," she said. She looked around and nodded toward a lonely Baobab tree standing just outside the village. "Let's go there," she said.

They sat side by side against the large trunk of the tree. The tree's many thick branches twisted and curved in every direction over their heads. Buds were just beginning to appear on the tree, which would bloom and bear fruit when the rainy season arrived.

Shawn took Jessica's hand and held it. "I know I scared you," he started, "when I started talking back home about taking our relationship to a new level. I've thought a lot about that since then."

"Me, too," she said.

He studied her face, but she didn't look at him. He wasn't sure whether she meant to encourage him. "Jess," he said, "I'm crazy about you—"

"Shawn—"

"No, please let me say this. I'm crazy about you. I know I haven't always been the kind of guy you deserve, but I think I can be that guy. I'd like you to give me another chance. I'm not saying, take our relationship to a new level; I'm saying, I want a chance to start again. Just start again, start over, you know? I think I took some things too fast with you. I know that was a mistake. I know I need to give you time, and take a little more time to show you that I can be the kind of guy you deserve."

"Shawn—" Jessica started again, but she stopped.

Shawn watched her. She wasn't looking at him, but he saw a tear roll down her nose and drop onto her arm. She looked up at him, her eyes now filled with tears.

"I really—I really do care for you," she started, and Shawn felt a sensation, like his heart was sliding into his stomach.

"You don't have to make a decision right now," he said. "I'm just asking you to think about it." He felt his own voice quivering.

She shook her head. "I *have* thought about it," she answered. "I don't want to hurt you at all, but I've known for awhile that God's upset with me. I have to do what he wants me to do."

"So do I," he said. "But—"

"I can't, Shawn." She lifted her head and turned her tearful eyes to him. "I just can't be with you anymore. I'm sorry." She pulled her hand out of his grasp and stood.

He stood, too, afraid she would dash away before he could say more. "Okay, Jess," he said. "Okay." His vision blurred with his own tears. "I understand . . . I think. I don't want to let you go without telling you: I'm sorry. I didn't treat you the way I should have. You deserve someone who helps you get closer to God, and I know I didn't do that very well." He paused. "Maybe not at all."

She wiped her cheeks with both hands. "I have to go now," she said. She looked at him, then walked away.

Shawn watched her go, then sat down against the tree trunk, wrapped his arms around his legs, and cried.

✝✝✝✝✝✝✝

"CAN YOU HEAR ME NOW?" Ratsbane pressed his cell phone against his giant ant head and listened. He stood at his desk in the gloomy cavern devoted to Project TruthTwister.

After a few moments, he awkwardly hopped a few yards away and crouched on his gangly frog legs. "Can you hear me now?" Finally, after a few more moments, he drew back his arm and flung the phone against the far wall of the cavern where it exploded into tiny pieces just as the ape form of Nefarius stalked into the room.

Ratsbane uttered a string of foul language, cursing cell phones in general and his now-shattered phone in particular.

"It—uh, it's not the phone, Your Foulness," Nefarius grunted.

"What?" Ratsbane croaked. "What did you say? Are you saying that *I'm* the problem? Is that what you're trying to say in your oafish way?"

"N-n-no, no," Nefarius said. "I'm not saying that at all."

"Then what *are* you saying?"

The great ape lumbered closer to his superior. "It has nothing to do with the phone. It's the service. It's—it's hard to get good reception in hell."

Ratsbane glared at his assistant, but Nefarius seemed not to notice. "I need a new phone," Ratsbane said.

Nefarius said nothing.

"Where's your phone?" Ratsbane asked.

Nefarius looked as if he hadn't heard.

"I said, 'Where's your phone?'"

Nefarius's shoulders drooped, and he opened one of his large paws to reveal a tiny yellow cell phone. Ratsbane snatched it out of his fellow demon's hand, and dialed fiercely.

"It works better over by the plasma screen," Nefarius offered.

Ratsbane lumbered across the office and put the phone up to his head. "Answer the phone, you insignificant little—" He paused. "It's about time! Can you hear me now?"

He turned and faced the plasma screen, which focused on the Westcastle group's efforts on the school building. "Good," he said. "Where are you? What are your coordinates?"

He listened again for a moment then croaked at Nefarius: "The remote. Give me the remote!"

Nefarius located the device on Ratsbane's enormous desk and took it to his superior.

Ratsbane pointed the remote at the screen; instantly, the image began to rotate. He stopped when the screen showed Rankmeat's bizarre cow body and turkey head shadowing a human form through the village's assemblage of mud huts.

"I see you," Ratsbane said. He tilted his head and stared at the screen. "What are you doing?"

He listened and watched as the human form on the screen—the chief man of the village—arrived at the hut where the boys were lodged. He stopped at the doorway, said something, then stepped inside.

Ratsbane watched with fascination as the man came out a few moments later, peered around both sides of the hut and, seemingly satisfied that no one was nearby, circled the hut a few steps at a time, apparently weaving something through the strands of grass that composed the roof.

"What is he doing?" Ratsbane asked, his head still cocked to one side. Then he started nodding. "Rankmeat, you demon shish kebab, I *like* it! For once, you've done something wonderfully evil! Keep up the bad work!"

Ratsbane hung up. Despite a face that was totally useless for displaying or conveying emotion of any kind, his twitching mandibles somehow hinted at a diabolical smile.

"What is it?" Nefarius asked, holding out a hand to receive his phone.

Ratsbane ignored the gesture and hopped to his desk, laying the phone there. "Those Westcastle kids will be leaving tomorrow," he said. Then he added, with a sinister glint in his dark eyes, "Those who survive, that is."

† † † † † † †

"Dude, are you sure you're okay?" Jason sat next to Shawn as the group gathered for devotions under the Baobab tree—the same tree where Jessica had broken up with Shawn that afternoon.

Shawn nodded, but he knew Jason would see right through his assurances. He felt sick. He wasn't sure how he would make it through the coming week.

He watched as Liz Cunningham started their devotions with a carefully-chosen song and a prayer and then turned things over to Sarah and D.J. He tried to listen as Sarah and D.J. sat back to back on the ground and started reading something, but he found it nearly impossible to focus—until he realized that they were performing a skit, as if they were boyfriend and girlfriend.

Shawn realized that Sarah was pretending to write. She would say out loud what she was writing. It was clear that the paper D.J. was holding in his hand was supposed to be the letter she had written, except something was wrong.

Shawn forgot his own troubles as the drama between Sarah and D.J. unfolded. Sarah was pouring her heart out to her boyfriend in the letter, telling him all sorts of things about her, things that anyone who truly loved her would surely want to know. But D.J. wasn't even reading the letter he held. He had his other hand pressed against his cheek, as if he were talking on a cell phone, but he wasn't talking to his girlfriend. He was talking to someone else, and he was actually admitting that he hadn't really read her letters!

"Remember," Sarah said, as she feigned writing, "how I wrote to tell you how sick I was? Well, one of the guys in my lab sent me flowers and a card. Wasn't that sweet? I would rather have heard from you. That would have meant so much to me. You might think it's silly, but I think it's so romantic when a boy sends flowers or takes the time to write a card or something like that. Those kinds of things really make me feel loved and cared for, but I'm sure you're busy."

As Sarah scribbled silently on the page, D.J. started talking to some invisible friend on his invisible cell phone. "Nah," he said, "she doesn't go in for all that flowers-and-candy kind of stuff. That's one of the great things about her. She's not romantic at all. She's really kind of unemotional."

Shawn watched, fascinated now, as the simple drama played out in front of the group. Sarah's character would write one thing to her "boyfriend," revealing herself—her dreams, her fears, all sorts of stuff. D.J.'s character would talk as if he knew her, though everyone who was watching could see clearly that he had no idea what he was talking about.

"Read her letters, stupid!" Shawn said out loud, forgetting himself.

The characters—and everyone in the group—looked at Shawn for a moment after his unexpected outburst. Alison giggled softly, but Sarah quickly grabbed everyone's attention by continuing the skit.

"I hope you don't mind me sharing all this," she said, still pantomiming the act of writing, "but I wanted to share my heart with you. I think it's important for you to hear all this because I felt like my last boyfriend created a fantasy girl that I could never live up to rather than discovering the person I really am. I don't want that with you. I want us to know each other for who we really are because that's the only way we can truly grow closer."

Sarah and D.J. stopped speaking, held still for a moment as if imitating a movie freeze-frame, then leaped to their feet and bowed dramatically as the group cheered their efforts.

Liz stepped in front of the group. "So," she said, "what was going on in that little skit?"

"The story of my life," said Darcelle. Everyone laughed.

"Well," Alison offered, "he was totally clueless."

"Like all guys," Sarah teased. Jason, who was sitting between her and Shawn, pinched her on the arm.

"It was a breakdown in communication," Alison said. "She was writing him letters so they could get to know each other, and he wasn't even reading them!"

"Do you think Sarah's desire for D.J. to truly know her was unrealistic?" Liz asked.

"No!" Shawn answered. "All he had to do was read her letters and pay at least a little attention."

"Yeah." Ryan spoke for the first time. "Everyone wants to be known, you know, for who they really are."

Liz nodded. "Do you think God is any different?"

The question stopped the group cold. No one answered for a few moments. Jessica, who hadn't spoken yet, said, "No, I don't think so. I think—oh, I see."

Everyone was looking at her. Liz was smiling. "What do you see?" Liz asked.

"The skit. Sarah is sorta like God, who's written us all sorts of things about himself, wanting us to know him, really know him, for who he is."

"And we're kinda like D.J.," Jason added. "It's like, God goes to all this trouble—revealing himself to people, inspiring them to write down his Word, preserving it for century after century, and eventually guiding the church in compiling it into the Old and New Testaments—so we can know him, and we're not paying any attention to what he really says about what he's really like."

Liz nodded. "No matter what D.J. believed about Sarah, he wasn't really getting to know her. He was more or less creating what he wanted to believe about her on his own, rather than discovering the truth about her—who she really is—which she was freely offering to him in her letters."

"So," Shawn said, "you're saying we do that with the Bible, right?"

Darcelle nodded vigorously. "Absolutely! We don't read it, or if we do, we don't pay attention to what God's telling us about himself all the way through it. We read it as just so much information, or so many commands, or stuff like that. But it's not meant only to be read and studied and preached and all that. It's supposed to draw us closer to God by showing us who he really is and what he's really like."

"I guess," said Ryan, "that's why I've heard my friends say things like, 'I think God just wants us to have fun all the time,' or 'I don't believe a God who really loves me would ever let me go to hell, no matter what I did.' When we don't read what he says about himself, we're bound to come up with all sorts of wrong ideas about him."

"So, let me get this straight," Jessica said. "The truth about God and who he is and what he's like has been written down for us, like Sarah's letters were written down. We have to make sure we're discovering the truth and not making it up, or we could be as wrong about God and what he's like as D.J. was wrong about Sarah and what she was like. Right?"

Liz nodded. "Right. Truth must be discovered not created. Which is why God gave us his Word, the Bible, in the first place."

The discussion continued for a few more minutes before Duane closed in prayer and dismissed everyone to his or her hut. Jessica didn't hear most of it. She was too busy thinking.

† † † † † † †

"YOU IDIOT! You rancid beefbag! You wattle-headed, pea-brained, cow chip factory!" Ratsbane screeched into his cell phone, his black button eyes bulging as if they would explode and his slimy green body quivering like Jell-O. "Can't you see what you've done? You've let that—that gaggle of giddy kids see right through Project TruthTwister! I've spent months plotting these kids' ruin, honing the program to perfection, tweaking every nuance, coordinating every move, and here you come along—one measly, foul-smelling, bumbling, incompetent demon assigned to do one, simple little task, and you bring the whole thing crashing down. I can't believe it!

"Do you realize the poison those two leaders poured into those kids' heads tonight? Now the idea is dawning on them that the Bible reveals the loving heart of that God of theirs. Not only that, they've been pounded with the idea that the Bible means what it says and not what they want to think it says. You've let that insidious pair of Bible thumpers throw a big-time wrench into the gears of Project TruthTwister, and you just stood by like a slab of frozen beef and let it happen."

"But—but what did I do?" the plaintive gobble of Rankmeat crackled over the phone. "Can I help what they say? It's not my fault that you let people like Duane and Liz lead this group."

"Ohhhhh, so it's *my* fault, is it?" Ratsbane's croak took on a deadly growl. "That's it. You've had it, you gobbling gangrenous gasbag. When you get back down here to the lower regions, it's the sulfur pits for you. Do you hear me? The sulfur pits!"

"Noooo! Pleeeze! Anything but the sulfur pits," Rankmeat pleaded. "All is not lost yet, Your Lowness. Don't forget what I've got set up to happen to these kids' huts. It'll work. I know it will. Soon they'll be nothing but piles of ashes. You'll see."

After a long moment, Ratsbane sighed. "All right, you get one more chance. I really don't have much choice, do I? I've got to work with the incompetents the lower management gives me. But this contrived plan of yours had better work or you'll soon be spending the rest of your eternity wheezing with brimstone lung. Do you hear me now?"

"Oh, thank you, thank you, O miserific one. My plan will work. Just keep watching."

Ratsbane slammed the phone to the table—causing Nefarius to cringe—then put his ant head in his sticky hands and sighed in frustration.

† † † † † † †

"How are you doing?" Sarah whispered to Jessica as they paused in the doorway of their hut. Somehow, Alison had not only beaten them there after devotions but seemed to be asleep already. It was clear that Darcelle wasn't far behind.

"What do you mean?"

"You know," Sarah said. "With you and Shawn breaking up." Jessica had shared the news with Sarah almost as soon as it had happened.

"I feel terrible," she said.

"For him or for you?"

Jessica thought for a moment before answering. "Both."

"Do you need to talk about it?" Sarah asked.

Jessica shook her head. "No. Thanks, though."

"You sure?"

She nodded.

"Good," Sarah said, smiling and rubbing her hand up and down her friend's arm, "because I'm exhausted! I'm going to be asleep before my head hits the pillow."

"You go ahead," Jessica said. "I think I just need to think."

"You . . . think?" Sarah joked. She patted Jessica's shoulder. "Promise to tell me if you need me?"

She nodded. Sarah disappeared into the hut, but Jessica remained outside alone. But it wasn't Shawn who occupied her thoughts. It was God.

Shawn lay awake in the boys' hut, his mind racing. He could hear the even breathing of the other boys nearby, and he assumed they were all asleep.

He had tried to pray for some time, but he was struggling to focus his thoughts enough to do that. His mind jumped back and forth between his heartbreaking conversation with Jessica and the topic of that night's devotions—especially the skit Sarah and D.J. had performed. He had never given any thought to the truth of the Bible. It had always seemed totally unimportant to him. That evening's devotions had brought up ideas that made total sense to him now that he stopped to think about them.

Shawn's thoughts were arrested by someone in the hut. Whoever it was stood for only a moment in the darkness before padding through the door and out into the night. After a few moments of tense silence, Shawn heard his name.

"Shawn?" It was Ryan's voice. "Are you asleep?" he asked.

Shawn shook his head without realizing that Ryan couldn't see him. "No," he added.

"Did you see that—someone just going out the door?"

"Yeah, who was it?"

"I think it was Duane," Ryan answered. "What do you think he's doing?"

"I don't know. I'm not sleeping anyway, so I might as well find out."

"I'm with you," Ryan said.

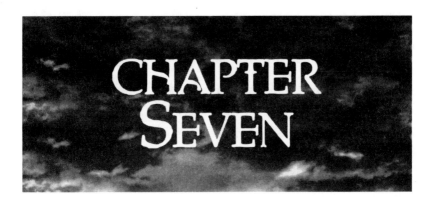

CHAPTER SEVEN

Shawn and Ryan stepped carefully in the darkness, trying to avoid disturbing D.J. and Jason who slept on thin mats between them and the doorway. Once outside, they heard rustling on the other side of the hut. They walked in the direction of the sound.

Duane immediately stopped what he was doing. "What are you guys doing out of the hut?" he whispered, his hands grasping something in front of him.

Ryan looked at Shawn then back at Duane with a shrug. "We wanted to know what you were doing."

Duane didn't respond immediately. He seemed to be thinking.

"So," Shawn prompted him, "what are you doing?"

"Okay," Duane said, "I'll explain it in the morning, but right now you guys can just help me with this and then we'll all get back to bed. All right?"

"Help you with what?" Shawn asked.

Duane tugged slowly, pulling something out of the straw roof of the hut. He extended it in the boys' direction. It looked like a length of copper wire.

"What is that?" Ryan asked.

"It's wire," Duane explained. "It's woven through the straw in the roof. I just need to get it out, that's all."

"Why?" Shawn asked.

"I'll explain tomorrow, okay?" Duane said. "Just get over here." He nodded to his right, where the wire still lay buried in the roof. "And be careful. I don't want to take a chance of breaking the wire; if we lost the end, it would be really hard to find it in the dark."

"And you want us to do this without pulling a whole section of the roof off, right?" Shawn added.

"Yeah," Duane said. "That's the idea."

A scream suddenly pierced the night air, and all three of them froze in their tracks. It came from only yards away. In the girls' hut.

Jessica heard the screams before she opened her eyes. She sat up, immediately wide awake, and saw the shadowy figure reaching out to grab her. She realized the screams were coming from her.

"Get away!" she screamed. "Get away from me!" She thrashed and clawed at the dim form in front of her and felt something talon-like closing around her wrists. She could no longer move her arms, so she scrambled to get her feet under her so she could run away. Another voice joined her screams. She thought it was familiar, and she tried to listen.

It was Liz—Liz Cunningham, her youth leader. Liz called her name, loudly, firmly, repeatedly. Drenched with sweat, Jessica blinked and saw that the form she was fighting also belonged to Liz. Liz gripped both of Jessica's wrists in her hands.

Jessica blinked again and saw beyond Liz. Darcelle, Sarah, and Alison all stood or knelt around them. Jessica could see their wide eyes gleaming even in the dim interior of the hut.

"Oh," she said. "Oh," again as she understood that she had been dreaming. She remembered the horror of the dream and collapsed in Liz's arms, crying.

She felt Liz stroking her sodden hair, rocking back and forth, and whispering, "You're safe now. It's over." After a long while, Jessica straightened and shifted into a sitting position.

"Are you all right?" Sarah asked.

Jessica wiped her tears and tried to focus on Sarah's face. "I—I had a nightmare."

"Yes," Liz said. "We know. Did you know that you were screaming?"

Jessica nodded. "Yeah. I'm sorry."

"It's all right," Liz said. "Do you want to talk about it?"

Jessica looked around. She had no idea what time it was or how long they had all been asleep. She felt badly for waking everyone. She noticed Duane standing in the doorway and felt even worse.

"Did I wake everyone up?" she asked.

"No," Liz answered. "Duane was already awake." She lifted her gaze to her husband. "I think she's all right, honey. You can go back to bed."

Jessica didn't hear Duane answer, but she knew he had gone. She closed her eyes for a moment. Her heart was still beating so hard; she felt sure the others could hear it. "What was I saying?" she asked.

"You were just screaming, like you were really scared," Alison said.

"I think I heard you saying, 'Get away,'" Darcelle offered.

"Do you want to tell us what you were dreaming about?" Liz asked. "Or would it be better if we talked about something else?"

Jessica shook her head. She felt the tears coming back, and she started to shake.

"Girl, you're still scared, aren't you?" Darcelle asked.

Liz wrapped her arms around Jessica once more and held her while she cried for a few moments. "Go ahead," Liz said. "Let it out. It's okay to cry."

Liz's words seemed to turn on a faucet somewhere inside Jessica, and the tears came full force, one wave after another, until she began to worry that it might continue all night—and maybe all the next day. No one seemed impatient with her or anxious to get back to bed. They all just sat with her. They would cry when she cried and stop when she stopped.

Finally, when she thought she could speak without totally losing control, she decided to tell them about her nightmares.

† † † † † † †

RATSBANE STARED at the monitor on the wall of his office cavern and watched as Duane, Shawn, and Ryan gingerly pulled the last strand of copper wire from the straw roof of the boys' hut. Nefarius's cell phone rang—an old song by the apish demon's favorite singers, Captain and Tennille. Ratsbane snatched it from the desk.

"Brilliant plan, you mangy meathead," he croaked snidely. "It didn't even take one night for your little brainstorm to fall apart, did it?"

"It can still work," Rankmeat's quavering voice answered. Ratsbane glared at the plasma screen and saw the underdemon standing helplessly by while Duane wound the wire into a tight coil and disappeared into the boys' hut with Shawn and Ryan.

"How can it still work?" Ratsbane bellowed. "It's a total failure."

"No," Rankmeat gobbled. "There's still the strip of sheet metal hidden in the thatch. That could still do the job."

"What's leaning next to the doorway of the girls' hut?" Ratsbane said.

"Girl's h—" Rankmeat's words choked off with a gulp. "Oh no, I guess I missed that."

"I guess I missed that," Ratsbane echoed in his best satire of Rankmeat's voice. "You're a total Dilbert, you know that? If I hadn't scraped the bottom of the barrel already, I would pack you off to the sulfur pits right now! Not only did your scheme not work, now that Cunningham fellow knows all about it! And he—"

Suddenly Ratsbane froze. *That Cunningham fellow knows all about it.* The thought played itself again in his head. *Yes! Maybe all is not lost yet.*

"I'm sorry, Your Impiety. I really—"

"Quiet!" Ratsbane croaked. "Don't say another word! I need to think. Wait! I've got it!" Ratsbane's words bounced off the cavern walls.

Rankmeat waited on the other end of the line, staring at the strip of sheet metal that had been removed from the boys' hut and wondering why he hadn't noticed it.

"Yes," Ratsbane said. "I think it'll work."

"What will work?" Rankmeat asked.

"It doesn't matter that your pathetic plan was discovered."

"It doesn't?"

"Death and destruction would have been nice, I give you that," Ratsbane said. "But they're hardly necessary to accomplish hell's purposes. Danger and fear will work just as well."

"They will?"

"Of course! But only a superior intellect like mine can manipulate these subtleties. I'll handle this from here. Remember, I'm an Ignoble Prize winner!"

"But—but how will you get rid of these Westcastle kids, Your Vileness?" Rankmeat asked.

"Just do what I say, you pitiful piece of poultry, and they will be on their way home first thing tomorrow."

"They will? How?"

Ratsbane didn't give his underling the pleasure of an answer. If it had been possible for him to smile, he would have. If he could have cackled, he would have done that, too. As it was, he wagged his bulbous head back and forth as if he were listening to music no one else could hear. *The reason it doesn't matter that Cunningham discovered the wires,* he thought, *is that he now knows he has reason to fear for his kids' safety. All we have to do is fan that fear and he'll pack up and leave.* The demon's jet black eyes glistened, even in the poorly-lit cave. Something flashed on the plasma screen.

"What was that?" he croaked.

"What was what?" Rankmeat said.

"That—" Ratsbane said. He pointed a froggy finger at the screen. "I saw blue! A blue-white light coming from *that* hut." He pointed to the girls' hut. "Noooooo!" he screeched. "We've been watching the wrong hut!"

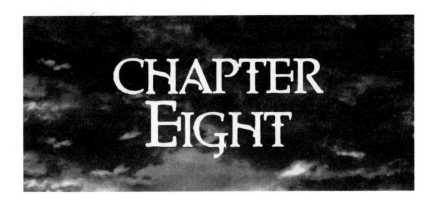

CHAPTER EIGHT

"Take your time," Darcelle told Jessica. They all sat around Jessica in the darkness of the women's hut.

Jessica inhaled deeply then exhaled slowly. She wasn't sure she could do this, but she mustered up the courage to tell her friends that she had been having horrible nightmares since she was too young to remember.

"When I was little," she said, her voice quivering, "my father used to punish me whenever I was bad."

No one said a word or made a move for a long time. Jessica was glad it was dark inside the hut.

"He would fill the bathtub—." She felt the fear rising in her chest and she thought she might throw up. She paused for a moment, took another deep breath, and continued. "He would fill the bathtub, make me get in it, and he would . . . he would hold me under the water . . . to teach me a lesson, he said."

"Oh, Jess," Sarah said.

"He would hold me under for the longest time," she said. Tears streamed down her cheeks. "I would hold my breath as long as I could until I felt like I would explode, but he always held me down longer. Sometimes I would swallow water; I couldn't help it. Sometimes I would pass out. Struggling only made him madder, so I tried not to fight back. After awhile, though, I just wanted to breathe. I was afraid I would die under there, and no matter how hard I tried, I couldn't stop being a bad girl."

Jessica noticed that Darcelle, Liz, and Alison were all crying. She couldn't see Sarah's face, because Sarah had moved beside her and wrapped her arms around her friend. Jessica knew Sarah was crying, too.

"How long did this go on?" Liz asked.

Jessica shuddered then shrugged. "I don't know how old I was when it started, but it goes back farther than I can remember. It lasted until—until my mom and dad divorced when I was seven."

"Oh, Sweetie," Liz said, "I'm so sorry."

"Me, too," Alison said. The other girls nodded.

"My mom said—." She stopped as fresh sobs rose in her chest. "My—my mom said that was why she had to divorce my dad. She did it," her voice was tiny now, "to protect me."

The group fell silent, except for an occasional sniffle.

Liz reached with both arms and grasped Jessica's shoulders in the dim light. She leveled a tearful gaze at her and said, "Jessica, I am so sorry for all you've been through."

Even in the dusky room, Jessica could see Liz's tears glisten as they rolled down her cheeks.

"I want you to listen as carefully as you can," Liz said, "and try to hear what we're saying. Do you think you can do that?"

Jessica nodded slowly.

"It is not your fault that your parents divorced," Liz said, speaking slowly and carefully enunciating each word.

Jessica inhaled fitfully, her breathing punctuated with tiny sobs. She blinked repeatedly, not only to blink the tears out of her eyes but also to focus intensely on Liz's face in the near darkness.

"And I am so sorry," Liz continued, "that you've had to carry that burden all these years."

A new wave of sobs wracked Jessica's body, and her shoulders shook violently with the emotion. Liz didn't sound surprised at all as she continued talking, slowly and clearly. “And I’m sorry that you were abused like you were, Jessica. I’m so sorry for that little girl who was afraid of being drowned by her own father, who lived in fear, who felt like she had no one to save her or protect her, who felt like she was a bad girl. I so hurt for you.”

“I do, too,” Darcelle added. “It makes me so sad to think of you being so hurt and so scared for so long.”

Sarah started to open her mouth to speak, but no words came out. She simply laid her head on her friend’s shoulder and cried out loud.

“Me, too,” said Alison. “I feel hurt just thinking of what you’ve been through. I—I wish it had never happened to you. I’m so sorry.”

The group of girls huddled around Jessica, crying for her and with her. She didn’t know how long they sat like that, but eventually she closed her eyes and laid her head in Sarah’s lap. She let her friend wipe her tears and stroke her hair. A short time later, Jessica drifted into peaceful sleep.

† † † † † † †

“YOU BLUNDERING BOVINE!” Ratsbane shouted into the cell phone. The girls’ hut glowed with an ethereal blue-white light.

“Wha—” Rankmeat gobbled, staring at the sight. “What’s going on?”

Ratsbane grabbed the remote control, pointed it at the plasma screen, and furiously punched buttons with one of his frog hands while still holding the cell phone against his oversized head with the other. “They’re brigadiers, you fool!” he screamed.

“Briga—what?” Rankmeat said. “Sounds sorta like a candy bar to me.”

“There’s nothing sweet about these things! I’ve done battle with them before.”

The blue-white light ascended in filmy tendrils from inside the hut, joining into twin columns above the roof. Ratsbane watched in horror as the light seemed to congeal into two large, muscular figures clad in sparkling blue and white uniforms. They circled in mid-air over the hut, arms spread, faces lifted toward the sky, performing a seemingly effortless dance of joy.

"Whoa," said Rankmeat, stationed just a few dozen yards away from the sight.

Ratsbane's frantic machinations seemed to have no effect on the events unfolding before his eyes. "These are the enemy's angelic light brigade," Ratsbane croaked, "invisible to humans just like you and me. But they are powerful, totally destructive to our cause." Ratsbane remembered a bitter confrontation with brigadiers back in the days of the Prime-Evil Impulse Transducer, or PIT as it was more commonly called.

"Where'd they come from?" Rankmeat, taking his cue from his supervisor, was shouting.

"Someone's been praying, you turkey! And you can be sure of something else." He punched a few buttons on the remote and the image on the screen split down the middle. The scene on Ratsbane's left was from inside the boys' hut, where Duane Cunningham sat cross-legged on the floor, praying, while the boys slept around him; the right side of the screen showed the inside of the girls' hut. "Ah! I knew it! That's what summoned the brigadiers!"

"What?" Rankmeat asked. He couldn't see the scene Ratsbane was witnessing.

"It's those cursed humans," Ratsbane said, focusing an angry gaze on Liz, Sarah, Alison, and Darcelle, who were huddled around Jessica, still crying and comforting her. "They're actually—they're—they're putting the enemy's Word into action, that's what they're doing!"

"How? Where?"

"If you weren't a total moron who's good only for the ash heaps and sulfur pits, you'd know! Look at them!" he bellowed. "They're weeping with *that one—*," he pointed the remote at Jessica, "as if her pain is their pain and her hurts are their hurts!"

"But—but don't people cry all the time?"

"Yes, but this is different. This isn't mere crying. That wouldn't be a problem if it were. This is actual, real, honest-to-goodness comfort, like the kind the enemy's Word talks about! Those humans are putting the enemy's teachings into action! They're not just talking about his Word; they're not just teaching it; they're not just studying it; they're putting it into action! To make matters really worse, when they do that you-know-who himself enters the picture." Ratsbane shuddered involuntarily. "All that comfort you see those kids giving each other . . . that's the clue. If you weren't so stupid you'd be shaking in your boots. What's happening, you slobbering idiot, is that God himself is inside those kids in the form of what he calls his Holy Spirit. You do remember what you read in Enemy Studies 101, don't you? And what our archenemy you-know-who promised in John 14? No, you were probably pulling the wings off flies instead of doing your homework. Since you are obviously too dense to see it, let me spell it out for you: These kids are actually connecting with God. This is the very sort of thing you are supposed to prevent, at all costs!"

"I still don't understand," Rankmeat said.

"Of course you don't," Ratsbane said, slumping against his desk as he watched Jessica close her eyes and lay her head on Sarah's lap, apparently exhausted from crying. "It takes a better brain than yours to understand. These Westcastle kids have picked up on a lot more than I thought. The only thing we can do about it right now is wait for the brigadiers to leave and try to mop up the mess."

✝✝✝✝✝✝✝

(THE INSIDE STORY)
ACTION NEWS

Pardon us for agreeing with a demon in hell, but Ratsbane is right. Liz Cunningham and the others are actually putting God's Word, the Bible, into practice. The comfort Jessica is experiencing in that hut in Mali is just one example of what happens when we don't approach the Bible as just a set of teachings or a collection of inspirational thoughts, but as a means of experiencing God and practicing righteousness. You see, the Bible really does mean what it says. It really does mean that God knows us, identifies with our problems, and actually gets personally involved in them. In John 14:16, the chapter that Ratsbane mentioned, Jesus promised his disciples that when he left, he would not leave them alone. God would very soon come again, and this time he would not merely be *with* them, he would actually be *inside* them in the form of his invisible Holy Spirit. That's the connection with God that the Bible promises. God in us gives us power to live as we should. He gives us insight and discernment into his truth. He gives us assurance and counsel and comfort—if we will simply become aware of his presence and submit our lives to his leading.

When I was a young Christian, I thought that the Lord was too perfect to associate with our human feelings. For years I felt that he was a stainless steel God—radiant, pure, and invincible, but without feelings. But as I read the Bible and got to know Jesus for myself, I made a startling discovery. I found out that Jesus has feelings. Not only that, I saw that he has feelings for *me!* I found, with great delight, that a favorite word to describe Jesus when he was on earth was "compassionate." Over and over again I noticed the Bible saying that Jesus had compassion for hurting, lonely, disconnected people. His love is not some impersonal, abstract, emotionless thing; Jesus is a warm, tender, gentle, kind, and sensitive person.

The Bible tells us in 2 Corinthians 1:4 that God "comforts us whenever we suffer" (GWT). He hears us when we cry (Psalm 18:6). He is attentive to our hurts and tears (Psalm 56:8). If you are hurting because of relational separation or loss, you need comfort from the compassionate Christ. And through prayer and God's Word, you can receive great comfort from God himself.

Of course, God lives not only in you but in other Christians as well. And he is pleased to share some of his compassion and comfort to all of us through each other. That is the delightful way God likes to work—through all of us who submit to him so that we can enjoy connections with him not only directly but also through each other. So God's Word tells us to "comfort [others] by using the same comfort we have received from God" (2 Corinthians 1:4, GWT). And his Word also tells us what comfort looks like: "Rejoice with those who rejoice, and weep with those who weep" (Romans 12:15, NASB).

That's exactly what we've seen Liz and the others doing for Jessica in the scene in the girls' hut. Under Liz's compassionate and sensitive leadership, they're experiencing just one aspect of what happens when we draw close to God through his Word and put into practice the very practical, relational realities we learn from him.

For example, notice through Liz and the others' example what biblical comfort looks like. Notice the words they spoke—and didn't speak. Notice that they didn't do a lot of talking at the beginning. Notice, too, that when they did talk, they resisted the temptation to offer glib, spiritual-sounding platitudes or even well-intended Bible verses. Instead, they focused on simply feeling what Jessica was feeling: weeping "with those who weep" as the Bible puts it (Romans 12:15, NASB). They said things like, "I'm sorry," "I so hurt for you," "It makes me sad to think of you being so hurt and so scared," and "I wish it had never happened to you." Those are words that convey true, biblical comfort to a hurting person. Those kinds of sentiments are an accurate reflection of Romans 12:15

and 2 Corinthians 1:4. And they are a perfect example of experiencing the Word of God by putting it into practice.

Of course, Jessica doesn't yet know that all of that was happening in the girls' hut. She doesn't yet understand that she has unexpectedly experienced some of the amazing things that happen when God's Word not only flows into our minds, but God himself actually enters us and his love flows through our lives and out through our actions. She hasn't yet grasped that she's actually drawn closer to God in those emotional moments in the hut. Nor does she realize that her nighttime experience will pave the way for even greater discoveries soon to come.

CHAPTER NINE

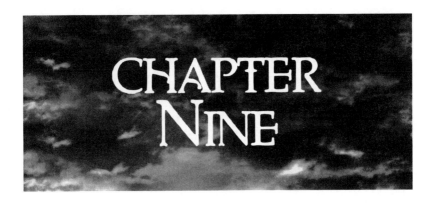

Jessica awoke. She didn't know how long she had slept, but it must have been a while because everyone else in the hut seemed to be sleeping soundly once more. She peered through the darkened hut in amazement. She'd never fallen asleep so easily or slept so soundly after one of her nightmares. In fact, they usually kept her up the rest of the night.

She lay on her back, listening to the sounds of the night. She thought she heard someone in the hut humming, so she sat up on her elbows and looked around, listening carefully. After a few moments, she laid back down and tried to go to sleep.

She heard it again, a soft melodic hum. She sat up once more, but even as she did so, she knew the sound wasn't coming from inside the hut. It was from somewhere outside.

Careful not to wake anyone, Jessica tiptoed out of the hut and quickly scanned her surroundings. She heard the tiniest rustling in the trees and saw only the outlines of the closest huts in the moonless night. She saw a tiny light and then a moment later heard the humming again, coming from the same direction. She walked slowly toward the light. She was nervous but strangely curious.

The light came from a tiny fire, stirred by an old—apparently ancient—African woman, who hummed a strange tune as she stirred the embers with a stick.

The woman lifted her gaze as Jessica approached and nodded slowly, as if agreeing with something Jessica had said (though, of course, Jessica hadn't said a word). They watched each other for a long time until the fire seemed tempted to go out. The old woman turned her attention to it and touched it with the stick, igniting a new flame from the coals.

Without knowing why she did it, Jessica folded her legs underneath her and sat cross-legged by the fire. She waited in satisfied silence until the woman spoke.

"Why are you not sleeping?" the woman asked.

Jessica stared at the woman as if she were seeing a ghost. "You—you speak English?"

The woman smiled and nodded. "You do not speak Dogon, do you?"

"N-no," Jessica stammered, still surprised.

"Then it is a good thing for me to speak English, no?" the woman said.

Jessica was still so surprised she found it difficult to respond.

"You have come a long way," the woman said.

Jessica finally found her voice. "Yes. From America."

The woman opened her mouth in a toothless grin. "I do not mean that. I mean inside." She pointed to her own chest, clearly indicating that she referred to Jessica.

"Why do you say that? How do you know that?"

"It is true, no?"

Jessica nodded. "Yes," she said. "It is true. I think it is, anyway. But how could you know?"

"You have been hurt," the woman said, "but your healing, it is begun."

Jessica peered intensely at the woman's face, searching her eyes in the flickering light of the tiny fire. "Who are you?"

"Your healing will help you in your search for truth."

Jessica continued to study the woman. *Maybe I'm dreaming this,* she thought. She turned and looked back at the way she had come. It didn't look like a dream. She turned again toward the woman and held her hands over the fire. It didn't feel like a dream.

The old woman spoke again. "You've been searching for 'the truth' inside you." It wasn't a question.

Jessica looked into the woman's eyes. She saw compassion and wisdom. She shrugged. "I guess so," she answered.

"But inside you carry so much hurt," the woman said. "And fear."

Jessica nodded.

"Do you think that hurt and fear will be a part of whatever 'truth' you create?"

Jessica crossed her arms in front of her and hugged them to her. She nodded. "Probably."

"Probably?"

Jessica lowered her gaze from the woman's face to the fire between them. "Okay," she admitted. "You're right. If I'm looking inside for the truth, and I'm all full of hurt and fear inside, then the 'truth' I'm going to come up with will have a lot of that hurt and fear attached to it. Is that what you're asking?"

The woman nodded slowly. She poked with the stick and guided a stray twig into the fire. "Is that why you think your heavenly Father wants to punish you?"

Jessica's head snapped up. Her eyes blazed brighter than the fire. "Who told you that?" she snapped. Her eyes narrowed.

The woman seemed unfazed by Jessica's reaction. "If you discover the truth instead of creating it for yourself, you will learn that your heavenly Father is very fond of you."

Jessica's eyes filled with tears. She was sure she was dreaming now, but she didn't want the dream to end. "What do you mean?"

"You think God is watching and waiting for you to make a mistake, and when you do, he will find a way to make you pay for your mistake."

A tiny sob escaped Jessica's throat. She nodded and closed her eyes against her tears, but the tears started to escape anyway, rolling down her cheeks. "Yes," she said, still nodding.

"Did you get that idea about God from his words to you?"

Jessica thought for a moment then opened her eyes, half expecting the woman to be gone. But she was still there, looking at Jessica, and awaiting an answer. Jessica shook her head. "No," she said.

"No," the woman echoed. "So what have you *discovered* about him from his words to you?"

Jessica thought for another long moment. "He loves me," she said. "He—he took my punishment away when Jesus died on the cross."

"Go on."

"He has good plans for me," she continued, remembering a Bible verse from somewhere in Jeremiah. "He wants good things to happen to me, things that will give me a hope and a future."

The woman nodded agreeably.

"He wants to have a relationship with me," Jessica said. "He wants me to know him—for who he really is. Not for who I think he is, or who maybe I'm afraid he might be . . . but who he really is."

A warm smile stretched across the woman's face. "Do you see," she said, "why it is so important to your loving heavenly Father that you *discover* the truth about him in his Word?"

Jessica nodded.

"His Word is his love letter to you. It is like a photograph containing his image. He wants you to know him as he is, as his Word reveals him to be. It is through his Word that you will see him more and more accurately. All your false ideas about him—ideas that come out of your hurts and fears, out of your past—will disappear, like a fire that has gone out. When you know who he is, understanding that he loves you dearly, you will want a relationship with him that is as intimate as your next breath. He offers that in his Holy Spirit. God himself wants to be the God inside you. The God of the universe wants to enter your life—literally—and become your permanent, loving companion."

The woman's words warmed Jessica as she sat in silence, watching the embers smolder. She sat that way for a long time, pondering the woman's wise words.

Finally, the woman spoke again. "Good night, my child," she said. She began humming the same strange tune that had coaxed Jessica out of her hut earlier that night.

Jessica gazed curiously at the woman's furrowed face. She stood and turned to go. "Good night," she said. "And thank you."

(The Inside Story)

How to Discover the Truth

That strange encounter with a woman in a West African village has helped Jessica to discover some of the many tragic consequences of trying to create our own "truth." Jessica has created a so-called "truth" about God based partly on her father's cruel treatment of her and her childhood traumas, including the divorce of her parents. She has formed ideas about who God is and what he's like out of her past experiences, not the things God has specifically, intentionally, tried to communicate to her in his written Word.

That's one reason it is so important for us to discover the truth in the pages of the Bible rather than "create" it from our own experiences, thoughts, and feelings. As Peter said, "No prophecy in Scripture is a matter of one's own interpretation" (2 Peter 1:20, GWT). If we don't seek to learn the objective meaning of a verse or passage of Scripture, we are effectively giving it our own interpretation. That is why we need clear guidelines for interpreting and applying what the Bible says, guidelines that will ensure that the image we see reflected in the pages of

Scripture is an accurate image of the God who wants us to know him. If we can do that, we spare ourselves the kind of heartache and difficulty Jessica has had in trying to relate to the heavenly Father who loves her.

This is so very important that I want to give you three simple, fundamental guidelines for interpreting the Bible that can help you make sure you're discovering the truth about God and his ways. You will find these guidelines at the end of this book in Appendix A.

CHAPTER TEN

The next morning dawned too quickly for Jessica. A tiny shaft of sunshine poked through the hut's roof and tickled her nose. She looked around and immediately saw that she was the last to awaken. Darcelle and Liz had already left the hut and returned to finish dressing before breakfast. Sarah sat cross-legged on her sleeping mat, brushing her hair, and Alison seemed like she'd been up for hours (but then, to Jessica, Alison always seemed that way).

"Morning, girl," Darcelle said. "How did you sleep?"

Jessica cocked her head to one side and smiled. "Pretty good." Her answer surprised even herself. She thought she should feel tired, the way she usually did after a nightmare incident. But she felt rested, even optimistic. "I hope you all slept okay. I mean, after I kept you up so late."

"You didn't keep us up," Sarah teased. "You *woke* us up!"

"Yeah, I did, didn't I?"

Liz pulled her hair back into a ponytail. "Do any of you realize what happened last night?"

Alison, Jessica, and Sarah looked at Liz with puzzled expressions. Only Darcelle seemed to see past the obvious answers to Liz's question.

"What do you mean?" Alison asked.

"Last night you saw in real live action what God's Word tells us," Liz said.

Alison echoed her own previous question, apparently without recognizing the repetition. "What do you mean?"

"Well," Liz explained. "You remember when Jessica's hurting started pouring out and she started crying?"

"Yeah," they answered, almost in unison.

"And when she cried, what did we do?"

"We cried, too," answered Sarah, as if she thought the question was silly.

Liz nodded. "Exactly. But why?"

"Well," Alison said, "because she was crying. We just couldn't help it."

"So," Liz said, smiling, "you felt sad because she was sad. You cried because she was crying, right?"

The group nodded together.

"Well, did you know you did exactly what the Bible says to do?" Liz said, adding quickly. "Does someone have a Bible handy?"

"I do!" Sarah answered.

"Good," Liz said. "Sarah, look up Romans 12:15 and read it to us, would you?"

Sarah turned the pages of her Bible and finally found the right page. "'Be happy with those who are happy,'" she read, "and 'be sad with those who are sad.'"

Liz nodded. "That's how the GOD'S WORD® *Translation* puts it: 'Be sad with those who are sad.' Other translations say something like, 'Weep with those who weep.' We did both of those things last night. We were sad because Jessica was sad. We cried because, when we saw her tears, we were moved to tears—which is the exact same thing that happened to Jesus at the tomb of Lazarus. The Bible says that when Jesus saw Mary and Martha crying, and all those who'd come to the funeral crying along with them, he was moved with compassion, and he cried, too."

"So," Darcelle said, "we were actually behaving like Jesus when we were comforting Jessica?"

Liz smiled. "Exactly."

"Wow," said Sarah. "That's pretty cool."

"Yeah," added Allison.

"Yes, it's cool," said Liz, "even cooler than you think."

"What do you mean?" Allison's question came a third time.

"Just this," replied Liz. "We were all moved to feel Jessica's hurt in the same way. God in the form of his Holy Spirit moved us to do it. You see, God loves us just as Jesus loved Mary and Martha. He is inside us, and he moves us to show his love and care to others in our own actions. He no longer walks on the earth in his own body as Jesus did; now he lives in the bodies of each one of us, and he expresses his love to all of us by moving us to love each other. That's why we all felt Jessica's hurt last night. We were expressing God's love and concern through our own actions."

The girls were silent for a long moment, awe and wonder showing in their eyes as the astounding truth sank in.

"Wow," Allison finally said. "That really *is* cool."

Liz turned her gaze on Jessica. "Jessica," she said. "How did you feel when all that was going on last night?"

Jessica thought for a moment. "I felt—I felt like I wasn't alone, maybe for the first time in as long as I can remember." She paused. She recalled the old woman by the fire, but she wasn't sure if she'd met the woman in a dream or not. She decided to wait before saying anything about the extraordinary encounter. "I do know last night was one of the strangest—and most wonderful nights of my life. This might sound weird, but I think something started to heal inside me. You know? It's like I started to get better last night."

Liz nodded. "That doesn't sound strange at all. That's what biblical comfort feels like. It's the first step in the healing process. Each of us experienced some of it last night. The Bible says, in 2 Corinthians 1:4, that when we have received comfort, we can then comfort others who are hurting with the very same comfort we have received.

We actually experienced the truth of God's Word last night. We experienced the love of God through our relationship with him—through the activity of his Holy Spirit in our lives."

Jessica's eyes opened wide. "I get it!"

"Get what?" Darcelle asked.

"I just realized—that's why the Bible is true!"

"What do you mean?" Darcelle asked.

Jessica's eyes sparkled. "I just figured it out. The Bible is true!"

Everyone nodded enthusiastically.

"You got that right," Darcelle said.

Liz suddenly froze. "Wait a minute," she said. "Back up just a little. What did you mean when you said, 'That's *why* the Bible is true'?"

"Well," Jessica said, frowning slightly in concentration. "When we find something that works, something that really works, like last night . . . Well, then, we can know we've found the truth! We can know the Bible is true because we've actually seen it work. You know?"

Liz nodded slowly. "You're right that last night we saw a demonstration of how the truth really works."

Jessica smiled.

"But," Liz continued, "I want to make sure we all understand that the Bible isn't true because it works."

Jessica glanced from Liz to Sarah, then back at Liz. "It's not?" she said.

Liz shook her head. "No, it's not. It's really important that we understand the difference between saying, 'The Bible is true because it works,' and saying, 'The Bible works because it is true.'"

"I'm confused," said Alison.

"I see what Liz is saying," Darcelle interjected. "It may seem like almost the same thing, but it's not."

✝ ✝ ✝ ✝ ✝ ✝ ✝

RATSBANE HOPPED over his gigantic desk in a single motion as if he planned to jump through the plasma screen and into the girls' hut in the Dogon village. He gripped the cell phone with all the strength in his ugly mutant body and screamed at it, holding it in front of his face.

"NOW!" he bellowed. "I don't care if you have to materialize in front of their very eyes and dance the Electric Slide, I want you to stop that conversation in the girls' hut right this minute! Not soon! Not as soon as possible. Not any minute now! I want it done IMMMMMEDIATELY!" He pressed the phone to his head, still shouting. "Do you read me?"

The voice on the other end crackled and sputtered in and out.

"What?" Ratsbane held the phone in front of his face and looked at the display for a moment before pressing it again to his ear. "What did you say? I couldn't hear you."

More crackles.

"Wait!" Ratsbane shouted. "Don't you dare hang up, you bucket of demon spit!"

He waddled a few feet to his right and looked at the cell phone display again. A stream of profanities emerged from his oversized ant head. He hobbled a few more steps before putting the phone to his head once more.

"Can you hear me now?" he screamed.

He heard Rankmeat's voice loud and clear but gave him no chance to speak before cursing him in the most demonic language he could summon. Finally, he stopped screaming and said, "Do you hear me?"

"Yes, Your Repulsiveness," Rankmeat's voice answered calmly. "Please, just look at your screen."

Ratsbane lifted his gaze to the image on the wall. His panic subsided as he watched the onscreen action with increasing interest. "What have you done?" he asked. He listened briefly to Rankmeat's explanation before interrupting, rudely, of course. "It better work, you rancid protein buffet. It just better work or you'll soon be sniffing sulfur dust."

✝✝✝✝✝✝✝

(THE INSIDE STORY)
TRUTH WORKS

It's no wonder that the girls' discussion has Ratsbane so worked up. Liz, Jessica, and the others have started down a path of discovery that is crucial for anyone who wants to truly experience the God of the Bible and follow him "in spirit and truth" (John 4:23, GWT).

Most people today—including young people—are very pragmatic. We want what is real, relevant, and "right now." We place a premium on finding our purpose in life and enjoying meaningful relationships—not only with each other, but also with God.

The problem, however, is that most of us have become convinced that what is true and relevant is whatever works right now. The culture all around us promotes the view: "If it works, it's right for you." In fact, according to research, 72 percent of teens believe "you can tell if something is morally/ethically right for you by whether or not it works in your life."[3]

Often, this leads us to think that such important ideas as the absolute truth of God's Word or the things we believe about Jesus Christ are mostly unimportant. "What's the point?" we might say. "As long as it works for me, that's all I care about." Many of us tend to think, "Don't bore me with your rules, your values, or your belief systems. And don't tell me what to think. I'm supposed to figure out for myself what works in the real world."

---

[3] Barna, "Third Millennium Teens," 44.

But as Darcelle and Liz were starting to express to Jessica and the others, there is a gigantic difference between saying, "The Bible is true because it works," and saying, "The Bible works because it is true." There is a huge difference between what seems to work for the moment and what is true and right for all time. For example, what if cheating on an exam meant the difference between passing or failing; would it be okay to cheat because it works at that moment? What if lying to your friends might help you avoid a big argument; would you think it is better to lie? What if stealing could make life easier or better; would it be all right to steal? For many, the answer is, "Well, if it would work for me right now, it would be right."

Does that approach actually work in the real world? Not for long, it doesn't. In this cause-and-effect world that God created, his ways are what work. His ways protect us from harm. His ways provide safety and blessing for us. His ways work better than seat-of-the-pants pragmatism. When we try to fashion our own version of reality—and live outside of God's design for us—our misguided belief that "what works right now is right (for now)" will eventually lead us down a path of self-destruction.

It is important to understand—as Liz and Darcelle recognize—that the Bible, the Word of God, is true in an absolute sense. As King Solomon recorded, "Every word of God has proven to be true" (Proverbs 30:5, GWT). As King David sang, "There is nothing but truth in your word" (Psalm 119:160, GWT). And as Jesus himself prayed to his Father, "Your words are truth" (John 17:17, GWT). God's Word is true. And his ways work because his Word is true, not the other way around.

† † † † † † †

"Darcelle is right," Liz said. "It may seem—"

A male voice suddenly interrupted the conversation from just outside the doorway. The girls all turned to look, but the owner of the voice seemed to be standing just out of view, apparently to respect their privacy. When he spoke again, the girls all identified the voice as Jason Withers's.

"Sorry, ladies," Jason said, "but Duane asked me to let you know that there's an emergency meeting under the Baobab tree as soon as you can all get there."

Liz stepped into the doorway. "What's this about?"

Jessica and the others heard the puzzlement in Jason's voice as he explained, "He's not saying, but he's totally serious, I can tell you that. He asked me to come over and tell you as soon as I got up and dressed this morning, but he hasn't said a thing about what it's all about."

The doorway became swallowed up in shadows. Jessica saw a dramatic change come over Liz's appearance. She looked at Sarah, who had a better view out the doorway. Shock registered on her face as well.

"Sarah!" Jessica whispered. "What's going on?"

Sarah said nothing, but she motioned to Jessica to follow her to the doorway. Darcelle was already standing right behind Liz, and Alison stood behind them all, on tiptoes to see around everyone else.

"Good morning," Liz was saying. "Can I help you?"

Jessica looked past Liz. The village headman stood there, taller than any of them—even Jason—and next to him was Aya, the girl Jessica met the first day there. Jessica watched as Jason sidled slowly beside Liz, as if he intended to protect her from the head man.

The head man spoke rapidly—angrily, it seemed—and gestured at his daughter, who seemed tiny and vulnerable next to him. She stared at the ground and seemed to be trying to make herself even smaller than she was already, tightly clasping her hands together under her chin.

The sound of an engine and tires sliding in the dirt suddenly sounded behind the headman, and a cloud of dust drifted over to them. Through the dust, striding quickly to the headman's side from the white panel van, came Joe, the Malian guide for the Westcastle group. He nodded tersely at Liz, and then he started speaking rapidly to the headman, who answered Joe in the same angry tones he had used moments before.

After a few such exchanges, Joe frowned. He seemed to hesitate, as though he were trying to decide what to do. He must have come to a decision, however, because he turned and addressed Liz.

"The village chief man says he is very sorry," Joe began. "His daughter—" Joe paused and gestured toward Aya. "This is her. He says that she was discovered with something that belongs to one of you."

Joe sighed and turned to Aya. He spoke a few sharp words to her, causing her to look up at him with fearful eyes. Finally, Aya opened her fists, and there, displayed in her delicate hands, was the teardrop necklace Jessica's grandmother had given to her.

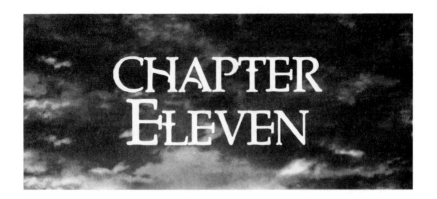

Chapter Eleven

"That's my necklace!" The words came out of Jessica's mouth before she even realized she was speaking. She looked from Aya to Liz to Aya's father then back to Aya, who hung her head and stared at the ground.

Joe nodded seriously. He turned and spoke briefly to the head man, who glared ferociously at Aya. "The chief man," Joe explained, "is concerned that his daughter's actions might have brought a curse on his village."

The chief man spat out a string of harsh-sounding syllables at his daughter and then turned and nodded at Jessica.

"He says," Joe interpreted, "that his daughter will return what she stole."

Liz leaned over and whispered in Jessica's ear. Jessica nodded her answer, which Liz relayed. "Joe," Liz said, "will you tell Aya and her father that Jessica forgives her and thanks her for returning the necklace?"

Joe froze. His forehead wrinkled as he seemed to be thinking deeply.

"Is something wrong?" Liz asked.

"It is just—" Joe said, "there is no word in their language that means 'forgive.'"

The girls all exchanged amazed expressions.

"No word for 'forgiveness'?" Liz asked. "Are you serious?"

Joe shrugged. "It is not an idea they understand."

Jessica asked, "Can you just tell them that I thank her for returning the necklace? Can you tell her it is a very important thing to me—that it was given to me by my grandmother, and I am very happy to have it back?"

Joe nodded. He turned to Aya and the chief man and spoke rapidly for a few moments. When he finished, the chief man snapped a few sharp commands to Aya, and she stepped forward with the necklace outstretched to Jessica.

Jessica smiled at the girl and reached out to receive the necklace. Suddenly, however, Aya stopped and clutched the necklace to her chest. Everyone watched, shocked. Her father broke the silence and reached for her. Without a sound, Aya eluded her father's grasp and dashed away, disappearing through the huts.

No one said a word until the chief man turned and stalked away. Joe's face wore a grim look.

"What do we do now?" Jessica asked.

Liz gripped Jessica's shoulder as she answered, "I guess we go to the Baobab tree."

"Dude, I'm starving," Jason told Shawn as they waited with Duane, Ryan, and D.J. under the Baobab tree.

Shawn nodded. "Duane," he said, "how long do we have to wait? I'm afraid Jason's going to waste away to nothing if he doesn't get some breakfast pretty soon."

"Yeah," added Ryan, "what's the big mystery?"

Duane opened his mouth to answer, but just as quickly shut it. Shawn followed Duane's line of sight and turned to see Liz and Darcelle, followed by the others, striding in their direction.

"What took so long?" Shawn teased.

"Yeah," Jason added, "are you ladies still looking for someplace to plug in your blow dryers and curling irons?"

Liz and Jessica's reactions made it clear that they were in no mood for such teasing. Liz briefly related to Duane, as the others looked on and listened in, a quick recap of the morning's events.

"So," Duane asked, "where is the chief man's daughter now?"

Liz shrugged. "We don't know. She took off pretty fast."

Duane nodded seriously. He turned his gaze on Jessica. "Are you all right?"

Jessica nodded.

He seemed to look at Liz for some reassurance. He apparently got what he was looking for, so he turned to the group. "Have a seat everybody," he said. "I'm afraid I have some unhappy news to share. We're going home."

"What?" Shawn asked. He looked at Jason, who merely nodded as if he had known what Duane was going to say.

"Last night," Duane explained, "I made a discovery that convinced me that we are less welcome here than we had thought."

"But we've barely gotten started!" Jessica protested.

Duane nodded. "Yes, I know, but I don't think it's safe for us to stay in this village another night."

"Why?" Shawn asked.

Duane sighed and met Shawn's gaze for a moment as he continued speaking. "Last night, Shawn and Jason helped me pull strips of sheet metal and strands of copper wire from the grass roof of our hut." He looked away from Shawn then looked around at the rest of the group.

"What's that mean?" Darcelle asked.

"It means that the chief man is far more antagonistic toward us than we thought."

"Why?"

Duane glanced quickly at Liz before continuing. "If there had been any lightning in the sky last night, it would have been easily drawn to the sheet metal and copper wire in our roof."

"You mean—" Sarah started.

"If our hut had caught fire, it would burn very quickly and the people in the village would conclude that we were evil and our project was cursed."

"But we took all the wire out," Shawn protested.

"Yes," Duane said, "but the danger remains. If the head man is trying to prove a point with copper wire, he will use whatever other means he has at his disposal."

Shawn saw Jessica shudder. "Are you all right?" he asked.

She waved a hand and smiled weakly at him.

"So," said Alison, "that's it? We came all this way for nothing?"

Duane started to nod, but Liz spoke next.

"No, not for nothing," Liz said. "We may not have finished our project, but God is still in control. He may be planning to do something even better than we had planned. We just don't know what it is yet."

Shawn studied Jessica, trying to gauge her reaction to the news. With Jessica and him newly broken up, he thought he probably should be happy at the prospect of this trip coming to an end. He didn't expect to have happy memories of this village, or of this spot under the Baobab tree. But while the others asked questions and chattered about this sudden change of plans, Shawn found something strange arising in him.

He stood. "Wait a minute," he said, surprising himself with his boldness. He could tell by the expressions on the faces of the others that they were surprised, too. "We came here because there's a whole village of people—a whole culture, right?—who don't know God. They're in the dark, and they don't even know it. We knew that coming in. We knew that we had to be careful. We knew that we would face challenges. We knew all that stuff and more, right? So . . . so maybe finding the copper wire and the sheet metal last night shouldn't drive us away. Maybe it should make us stay. Maybe it just shows how bad these people need what we came to show them!"

"Yes, it does," Duane said. "But this is a high school mission trip, and—"

"But," Shawn interrupted, "don't we need to show some courage? Shouldn't we care more about these people than we do about our own safety?" Even as he spoke the words, Shawn couldn't believe what he was saying. He saw Jessica studying him. He couldn't tell if she was impressed . . . or repulsed. Maybe neither. But he knew that he didn't want to leave this village, not this way.

"Shawn," Duane said. His face began to flush with color, and it wasn't from the rising heat of the late morning.

Shawn wasn't finished. "I mean, come on everybody," he said. "Do we really believe the things we say we believe? Do we really believe the Bible is God's Word? Do we really believe these people need Jesus?" He could tell his words were having an impact on some of the group—D.J., Ryan, Sarah, maybe even Jason. "Do we believe it enough to stick our necks out? If we don't—what are we doing here in the first place?"

† † † † † † †

(THE INSIDE STORY)
TRUTH MATTERS

Shawn's passion may surprise you. It is definitely surprising Duane Cunningham and the rest of the Westcastle group in Mali.

Whatever happens next, one thing is certain: It's times like these when it becomes crystal clear that truth matters. Since the Bible is the means God uses to bring us into his kingdom through the experience of salvation, then it matters whether or not it is true. Since the Bible is the primary means God has given to us by which we can enter into a relationship with him and get to know him, then it matters whether or not the Bible contains accurate information. If—like many others before us—we are going to risk anything in the service of God and his kingdom, then it matters whether or not we're putting our trust in a reliable document.

If Shawn, Duane, Liz, and the others don't have good reasons to believe that the Bible is trustworthy, they'd be foolish to risk so much as a parking ticket in order to share the Bible's message with others. If, as Shawn suggests, they don't really believe what the Bible says, then they've been foolish to travel thousands of miles to make the Bible available to others. If they don't have sound reasons to believe in the reliability and accuracy of the Bible, they would be utterly foolish to "stick our necks out," as Shawn so forcefully put it.

So, it's worth asking: Is the Bible accurate? Is it reliable? If it's not, then everything it may tell us about God's love for us, or his forgiveness of us, or his passion to have a relationship with us (Exodus 34:14, NLT) are just so many wasted words. If there's no good reason to believe the Bible is true in what it says, then there's no use serving God or sharing his love with others—or trying to experience it ourselves—because it could all be no more than wishful thinking. If the Bible is not an accurate revelation of God and his ways, it cannot truly or reliably lead us into a relationship with him, or to experience his forgiveness of our sins, or to find a meaningful purpose for our lives, or to experience many other things Christians claim the Bible shows them.

In light of all that, doesn't it make sense to take some time to investigate the Bible's accuracy and reliability? Absolutely! And when you do, right from the very start you will discover some amazing things that distinguish the Bible from all other documents of the ancient world.

The Bible was written during a fifteen hundred-year span through more than forty generations by more than forty different authors from every walk of life. It was composed in a variety of places: in the wilderness, in a palace, in a dungeon, on a hillside, in a prison, in exile. It was penned on the continents of Asia, Africa, and Europe and was written in three languages: Hebrew, Aramaic, and Greek. It contains hundreds of stories and songs, and addresses hundreds of controversial subjects.

Yet through it all, it achieves a miraculous continuity of theme.

Because I think it's so important that you understand just why you can trust the Bible to be reliable, I have summarized for you three important facts that are well established by careful research. These facts will give you powerful reasons to believe that the Bible is historically reliable and that its claims are supported by mounds of solid evidence. This material is short and easy to digest, and I have placed it at the end of this story in Appendix B. I urge you to spend a few moments reading this material. If you haven't encountered this evidence before, I think you'll be amazed at what you find there.

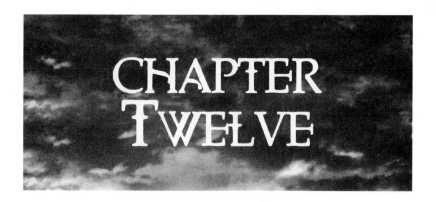

CHAPTER TWELVE

"Shawn, that's enough!" Duane said, his voice loud and firm. "That's a great question, and every one of us needs to answer it for ourselves. We answer it every day, in fact, by how we live our lives and share our faith—whether we're in school or at work or playing around with our friends.

"I'm proud of you for wanting to stay, even in the face of danger. It's a choice I hope we would each make, if we were making the choice for ourselves, as individuals. I don't have the luxury of making that choice only for myself. I'm the shepherd of a flock here, in a way, and I've been entrusted with the care of others. For some of you, I had to get your parents' permission to bring you here, and I have a responsibility not only to the people of this village, but also to you and to your parents. As much as I would love to see every single one of us decide to throw caution to the wind and risk our own well-being for the chance of having an impact on the people of this village, *I can't do that*. I have to do everything in my power to get you home safely."

Shawn felt himself blushing. He understood Duane's point, but he still struggled with the idea that their trip would end like this.

"Listen," Duane said, as if he read Shawn's thoughts. "I know it's a disappointment. I'm disappointed, too, but I'm making the decision. I'm taking the responsibility, and we're leaving today. As soon as we can pack out of here."

Shawn looked around. A wave of relief seemed to pass through the group, and he suddenly felt foolish. "Duane," he said, "I'm sorry. I—"

Duane clamped a hand on Shawn's shoulder. "I don't think you said anything you should be sorry for. I respect you for speaking up, and I hope I always feel as strongly about people who don't yet know the love of God. That's a good thing to be passionate about, Shawn."

Shawn smiled. "Thanks," he said.

Duane smiled back and nodded. Then he lifted his head and addressed the group again. "We have a long and dusty ride ahead of us," he said. "We'd better get packed up as quickly as we can."

† † † † † † †

"WHEW!" GRUNTED NEFARIOUS, the walrus-headed demon with a gorilla's body. "That was a close one!"

Ratsbane slumped into his desk chair and stared, exhausted, at the plasma screen on the wall. He had been working furiously during the entire meeting under the Baobab tree, the remote control in one hand and Nefarius's cell phone in the other. He was exhausted, but things had turned out well—horribly well. He watched with smug satisfaction as the Westcastle kids headed back to their huts, Duane and Liz walking arm-in-arm behind them, the whole group a picture of sadness. He slowly became aware of a mad cackling sound coming through the tiny speaker on the cell phone, which still lay open in his hand.

He lifted the phone to his ear and croaked weakly.

"What did you just do?" It was Rankmeat's voice on the other end of the line. "I don't appreciate being left out in the cold, you know!"

Ratsbane's bulbous ant head lolled around atop his frog torso. He sighed. "I'm too tired to argue with you, you worthless piece of road kill. You failed, and so I had to step in and handle things again. And as you can see, I got them done. It's the difference between high genius and gross incompetence. If you had a brain, I would say you could learn a few lessons from the way I operate. Since you don't, what's the point?"

"Your Esteemed Foulness, I did my best," Rankmeat cackled, "I tried every trick in the book, but for some reason not one of my shots landed. It wasn't my fault."

"If what you've been doing is your best, I'd hate to see you on an off day. No, you bubonic-beaked birdbrain, I'm afraid you're good for nothing but the sulfur pits after all. I'll have your shipping orders ready the moment you return."

The cell phone emitted a string of stricken gobbles and wails, which soon turned into a series of erratic crackles, followed by silence. Ratsbane flipped the device over and opened the battery compartment. Two slim batteries rolled onto his desk. "This thing must need new batteries." He snarled at Nefarius. "You should take better care of your equipment, you lopsided blubber head. Get me new batteries! Now!"

Nefarius lumbered out after the batteries, and Ratsbane slumped again into his chair. He was tired but pleased, or at least as pleased as a demon in hell can be. There had been some close calls, but Project TruthTwister had won the day. He would see that the official reports all pointed to his subordinates Rankmeat and Nefarius as the cause of all the bumblings, miscues, and near disasters that had brought the project to the brink of crashing. He would take care of that later. All he cared about at the moment was savoring his current victory. The Westcastle group was heading home where it would be easier to resume the diabolical deception of Project TruthTwister.

† † † † † † †

"I can't believe this is happening," Jessica told Sarah as the girls began to pack their things for the return trip.

Liz stood next to Jessica, packing her own bag. "It does seem unreal," she said. They worked in silence for a few moments, each of the five girls shoulder-to-shoulder in the small room. "But even when I don't have a clue what God is up to," Liz said, "I know he is working."

Darcelle nodded. "Jesus said, 'My Father never stops working.'"

"I wish I knew my Bible like you do, Darcelle," Sarah said. Alison and Jessica agreed.

"I wish I knew it like Liz does!" Darcelle said, smiling.

"I wish I knew it like Duane does!" Liz countered, and they all laughed. "And I know Duane wants to know God's Word more than he does, too."

Jessica nodded slowly. She felt the same way, and she was glad to know she was not alone. She stuffed a pair of socks into her bag and felt her bracelet. She pulled it out slowly and turned it around in her fingers.

Sarah must have noticed. "Oh," she said. She turned to Liz. "Jessica still doesn't have her necklace back from that girl."

Liz nodded. "I'm sorry, Jessica. I'm not sure we can get it back for you."

Jessica's eyes clouded with tears. "My grandmother gave these to me. I never should have brought them on the trip." She studied the bracelet again. "At least I still have this."

The boys' luggage was strapped to the top of Joe's van.

"Good work, men," Duane said.

"Should we see if we can carry the girls' things?" Shawn asked.

Duane looked out from between the back doors of the van in the direction of the girls' hut. "Sure," he said, "but you'd better hurry."

Shawn saw that the girls were heading their direction, canvas duffel bags slung over shoulders and other luggage hanging from their hands. He and the other guys jogged over to help, and moments later the van was loaded. The group clambered into the vehicle, and Joe slid into the driver's seat.

The air hung heavily in the van, not only from the heat of the midday sun, but also from the somber spirits of the group. Just yards away stood their unfinished building project.

Joe started the engine and began to pull away.

"Wait," Shawn said. Everyone turned to look at him. "We didn't leave behind a single Bible, did we?"

They looked at each other, and Liz finally answered. "Well . . ."

"Since we're leaving anyway, what could it hurt?"

"What could *what* hurt?" asked Alison.

"Can't we just—I don't know—get our Bibles out of our luggage, and leave them in the huts we stayed in or something like that? I mean, maybe the head guy will destroy them . . . but maybe not."

There was an awkward silence. Jason was the first to speak. "I actually did leave my Dogon Bible in the hut."

Duane looked at the others for a few seconds. Then he smiled. "I left mine under the Baobab tree."

"Me, too!" Sarah Milford said.

They started laughing, then, sharing the reports of where the Bibles had been left behind.

"Am I the only one?" Shawn asked. "Everybody but me left a Bible behind?"

"Not exactly, dude," Jason said. "I got your Bible out of your bag when you weren't looking. It's with mine back in the hut."

Shawn blinked a few times, then a smile broke across his face. "Well, all right!" he said.

Duane laid a hand on Joe's shoulder. "I guess we're ready," he said. "We've done all we can do here."

Joe started the engine. Dust rose around the van as he started driving. A low thrumming sound suddenly began in the distance.

"What's that?" asked Jessica.

"Is something wrong with the engine?"

Joe shook his head. "No," he said. "It's drums."

"Drums?" Jessica asked. "Really?"

Joe nodded seriously.

They all thought Joe would say something more. When he didn't, Shawn asked, "What are the drums for?"

Joe kept driving and seemed in no hurry to answer. Finally, he said simply, "They are for the girl."

"Girl?" Jessica asked. "What girl?"

He lifted his eyes to the dirty rear-view mirror hanging from the windshield. He studied Jessica's curious face for a moment. "The chief man's daughter."

Shawn saw Jessica shoot a look at Liz. "What's going on?" he asked.

Jessica didn't respond to Shawn, but she repeated her question to Joe. "What are the drums for?"

Alison, who was sitting next to Jessica, told Shawn, "The chief man's daughter stole Jessica's necklace."

"The drums call the village together," Joe said.

"When did this happen?" Shawn asked Alison, recognizing her as his best hope for information.

"For what?" Jessica asked Joe. "What are they being called together for?"

Alison shrugged at Shawn. "I don't know," she said. "We just found out this morning. The head man guy was pretty mad. And then the girl ran away with the necklace."

Joe hadn't answered yet. Jessica repeated her question. "What are they being called together for?"

Joe glanced quickly at Duane in the front passenger seat. Then he looked again at Jessica in the rear-view mirror. "She must be punished," he said.

"Punished?" Jessica repeated. "How?"

"In this village," Joe said. The van suddenly hit a hole in the dirt roadway, sending everyone jouncing around in the back. A moment later, this time with his eyes on the road instead of on Jessica in the mirror, he said, "It is a shameful thing to be caught stealing."

"How is she going to be punished, Joe?" Jessica insisted. By now the others in the van had become spectators, closely following the exchanges between Joe and Jessica.

"The chief man believes she must be cleansed," he said.

"Cleansed . . . how?"

"In the well."

"What do they do?" Jessica pressed him. "How do they clean her? Do they wash her with rags? Or pour buckets of water on her? What do they do?"

"The people in the village believe people steal because of evil spirits. Water will drive the spirits out."

"What do they do to her, Joe?"

"They will lower her down the well," he explained.

"Down?" Jessica asked, her tone rising. "Down in the well? How deep is the well?"

Joe shrugged.

"How long do they keep her down there?"

Another shrug. "I do not know."

"Do they leave her under water?"

This time he nodded. "If she lives, she will be cleansed."

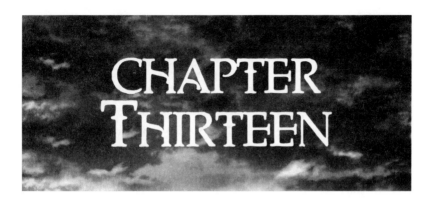

CHAPTER THIRTEEN

"If?" Jessica cried. "*If* she lives?"

Joe shrugged again. "She will probably be okay. She is the chief man's daughter."

Jessica turned to Liz, her eyes wide with passion. "Liz, we have to go back. You saw her father. You saw the look in his eyes."

Liz nodded seriously, but before she could say anything, Jessica turned to Duane. "We have to go back," she repeated.

Duane and Liz exchanged serious glances and then Duane nodded, too. "Turn us around, Joe," he said. He twisted in his seat to address the entire group. "This isn't a matter of our safety alone anymore," he explained. "It involves that little girl. Is everyone okay with going back?"

"You bet," Shawn answered. The others agreed just as enthusiastically, and Joe quickly turned the van around and headed back toward the village.

When the Westcastle group jounced into the village, it looked like the entire population had assembled in the center of town. The well was obscured from view.

Jessica was the first to exit the van, but the rest of the group was right on her heels as she pushed through to the center of the crowd. Over the nearly deafening sound of many drums, she heard Liz's voice behind her, shouting her name. Jessica knew that Liz wanted her to slow down, to wait for her, to be careful about bursting into the crowd of villagers. She couldn't stop, though, and the next moment she burst through the ring of people and stood face-to-face with the chief man of the village.

The sight of the chieftain's imposing figure and stern face momentarily stalled her momentum, and she felt Liz and the others catch up to her. Without looking, she knew that Liz stood at her left side. Shawn was standing next to her on the right, and the others were grouped around her. While she was aware of their presence, she had no time to look or say anything to them.

Aya stood quivering on the other side of the chief man flanked by a line of men sitting cross-legged in the dirt, beating the drums loudly, maddeningly. Aya stood on a wooden disk at the end of a rope suspended over the village well. Her hands, bound in front of her, gripped the rope tightly, desperately. Aya met Jessica's gaze, and Jessica recognized in her eyes an all-too-familiar expression, one Jessica supposed she had worn herself many times as a child. It was a look of terror and helplessness.

Jessica took a step in Aya's direction and addressed herself to the chief man. She felt Liz's hand grip her arm, but she spoke anyway. "Please," Jessica said, "please don't do this."

Suddenly Joe was in front of Jessica, his face close to hers. "It is not good, what you are doing," he said. "You are making things worse for the girl."

Jessica's eyes clouded with tears. "You don't understand," she said.

"No!" Joe interrupted. "It is you who do not understand. You cannot stop this. The more you say, the more you do, the more you will force the head man to stand his ground. You will make it much worse for the girl."

"But—" Jessica whispered, tears streaming down her cheeks.

"They will lower her into the water," Joe explained, his words coming out sharp and slow. "Three times."

"How long?" Jessica asked. She had to scream her question now, as the drumming seemed to get even louder and the chief man began to chant what sounded like angry words to the crowd. He cast a dark look at his daughter, who still stood shivering, clinging to the rope over the gaping mouth of the open well.

Joe shook his head. "I do not know." He, too, was shouting.

"But you said, '*If* she lives.' Back in the van, you said, '*If* she lives.'"

Joe nodded. "Stealing is a very, very bad crime to the Dogon people," he shouted. "Very bad."

A scream pierced the air, easily heard even above the wild thrumming of the drums. Jessica looked in Aya's direction; a man was unwinding the rope, apparently preparing to lower Aya into the well.

"Stop!" Jessica screamed. No one among the villagers paid any attention. It was as if she wasn't even there. She turned and looked to her friends who all wore horrified expressions.

Jessica felt the change in her face first. The fear in her expression left, and she felt a hardness, a determination take over. She pivoted, pinned her gaze on Aya's quivering form, and leaped across the distance between her and the chieftain's daughter. In an instant Jessica stood on the wobbling wooden disk and gripped the rope with Aya.

Jessica heard the shouts of her friends from Westcastle. The chieftain's voice rose to a new volume and intensity. She ignored them. She looked into Aya's eyes. She couldn't believe her own words when they escaped her mouth.

"If they're going to do this to you," she said, "they're going to do it to both of us."

"Jessica, no!" Shawn shouted as he watched Jessica dash toward the chief man's daughter. He took off after her but was pulled back by a quartet of strong arms. "Let me go!" he growled, struggling against his captors.

Jason and D.J. had grabbed him before he had taken two steps. Duane and Liz had stepped close to the chief man, with Joe at their side, translating their rapid words to him. The chieftain seemed unaware of their presence. He gazed into the sky and chanted louder and louder as the drums throbbed still faster and louder.

"What are you doing?" Shawn screamed at his friends. "Let me go!"

Jason shook his head seriously, resolutely. "No, dude."

"Why didn't you stop her?" Shawn shouted.

"I didn't know she was going to do that . . . but I knew you were."

Shawn turned, his jaws tightening and his eyes filling with tears. Jessica stood on the rope, precariously perched on the little wooden disk with Aya. Neither the rope nor the disk looked strong enough to hold even one of them, let alone both. "What's she doing?" Shawn asked, helplessness cracking his voice.

"I wish I knew," Jason said.

"I know you can't understand me," Jessica said. She and Aya stood cheek-to-cheek, clinging to the rope over the dark opening of the well. "Maybe they won't put us both down in the well." She tore her gaze away from Aya's eyes, red with fear and confusion, and looked around at the chanting, screaming, drumming crowd. She looked at the girl's own father, who was now looking into the sky over their heads. Her gaze finally settled on the man who gripped the rope; he was intently watching the chief man, clearly awaiting a signal.

Jessica was suddenly very sorry she had acted so impulsively. She knew her action—just as Joe had warned—would not forestall or delay Aya's fate. She knew now they would both be lowered into the well unless something drastic happened soon.

She put her lips close to Aya's ear. "Whatever happens," she whispered, salty tears streaming down both cheeks, "you won't have to go through this alone, like—like I did." She closed her eyes against the panic.

She was suddenly back home, the house she had lived in before her parents divorced. She heard water running and felt the familiar knot in her stomach. She felt like she was going to throw up, but there was no time. There was no opportunity, and she had no control. She felt a strong hand on her back, and another strong hand pushing against her chest, and she felt herself falling backward, into the tub, under the water, into the dark. The water rushed over her tiny form, filling her ears and her nostrils, and the humming started inside her head. She wanted to breathe, but she knew she couldn't open her mouth or the water would rush in there, too. She could hear her heart beating inside her chest, and her lungs started to burn. She started to fight to sit up, but still the hand held her firm. She wasn't strong enough; she was too small, too weak, too helpless. She fought, but the hand pushed harder the more she struggled. She finally just gave in and tried to lie as still as her panic would allow, waiting. Soon, she would no longer be able to hold her mouth closed, and the water would rush in and fill her lungs.

Shawn couldn't believe all this was happening. He'd never been so scared in his life. All those times that he'd put himself in harm's way now seemed like playing little children's games.

"What do we do?" he yelled at Jason. "What do we do?"

Jason, who still gripped Shawn by the arm, shook his head.

Shawn wrestled his arm free from D.J.'s grasp and gripped Jason's shoulder with it. "Do you believe that stuff—"

"What?" Jason asked, turning his head in Shawn's direction so he could hear him better.

"Do you really believe that stuff about those three Hebrew guys being saved when the crazy king threw them into that fiery furnace? Do you think that really happened?"

Jason looked confused. "What are you talking about?"

"Is it true—really true, I mean, not just 'true for me' or something weak like that—that God got in that fire with those three men and saved them? Is it?"

Jason blinked, still clearly confused. "Yeah, but—"

Darcelle spoke next, though neither Jason nor Shawn had known she was nearby, let alone that she had heard Shawn's questions. She nodded vigorously. "Yes," she said firmly, her usually soft voice inexplicably clear over the noise of the crowd and the drums. "It *is* true, true as true can be. It's not just true for you. It's true for everyone, for everywhere, and for all time. It's true right now and right here. God did deliver Daniel through the lions' den, and he delivered those three Hebrews from the fiery furnace. You can believe it. There's no reason to believe he can't do that now, if we pray! Right now!" She pointed a finger at Jason, Shawn, and D.J., in turn. "The best thing you can do right now is to pray. Pray for God to do for Jessica what his Word says he did for Daniel and the others."

The rope jerked, and Jessica forced herself to open her eyes just in time to see that she and Aya were slowly being lowered into the mouth of the well.

The panic washed over her like water, and she fought for control. Her gaze settled on Aya, screaming and weeping hysterically, and the fight was over. She let go of the rope with one hand and gripped Aya's shoulder. She mimicked the act of inhaling, puffing her cheeks out and exhaling slowly, right into Aya's face. The girl looked confused momentarily, but Jessica saw a flicker of comprehension in her expression just before the water covered their feet.

It was dark, and Jessica could feel the motion of being lowered deeper into the narrow well shaft and into the water that would soon cover their heads. As the shadows inside the well closed around them, Jessica suddenly heard a soft sound in her ears—the strange tune she had heard the old African woman hum just the night before. The tune seemed to fill her spirit and body with a supernatural calm. As frightened as she was, she remembered the words she had spoken to the woman: *God has good plans for me. He wants good things to happen to me, things that will give me a hope and a future.*

A moment later, she and Aya were under water.

As they rose, gasping for air in great frantic gulps, Jessica never took her eyes off the chieftain's young daughter. She knew that words were useless, but though she was fighting panic herself, she tried to communicate with her tone of voice the same kind of comfort she had received from her friends just the night before. She remembered the old woman's words and prayed that she would be able to comfort Aya with the comfort she had received from God through the compassionate words and tears of her friends.

As their heads cleared the well opening, Jessica knew they were visible to the crowd surrounding them, but she refused to tear her gaze away from Aya's face. She silently thanked God that the water from the well, streaming from her hair down her face, obscured the tears she couldn't seem to stop. She prayed for Aya to take some strength and comfort from her presence—even as she was finding strength in the realization that God was with her and Aya. He would not leave them as they endured another descent into the depths of the well.

She whispered, "I'm staying with you. You're not alone." She knew the words were unintelligible to Aya, but she watched with amazement as Aya nodded, and—as the rope shivered again foretelling their next descent into the well—lifted a single finger into the air.

Jessica nodded and attempted a smile. "You're right," she said. "One down. Two to go."

When the warm air outside the well hit Jessica's face, she opened her eyes. The sky seemed to be spinning over her head. She thought she might pass out. Then she thought she had passed out.

She coughed and spat water out of her mouth. She reached out to Aya, whose head lolled on her shoulders. Jessica touched her cheek and the girl jumped. She opened her eyes and looked at Jessica.

Relieved, Jessica flashed two fingers at Aya and forced a smile. "Two down," she whispered. "Just one more. We're almost done."

Aya nodded seriously, sadly.

Jessica felt a new wave of despair. *Nothing is holding us to the rope, and we are losing our strength. If one or both of us passes out and loses our grip, we could slip off the rope and stay in the well, even when the rope is pulled out.*

She inhaled as calmly and deeply as she could, and as she did, cast a glance over Aya's left shoulder . . . where she saw the old woman from the hut. The woman's expression was unsmiling, but her face shone with serenity. Jessica watched in silent amazement as the woman lifted both hands in the air in front of her, one cupped against the other as if they were folded in prayer—or tied together at the wrists.

Suddenly, Jessica remembered: Although Aya's hands were not bound to the rope, they were bound together! If she fell from the platform, she would not even be able to tread water to stay alive. The rope started to twitch with movement once more. She knew they were headed back down in the well. Jessica, fastening her eyes on Aya, lifted the girl's arms over her head and threaded her head, left arm, and shoulder through them in a crooked embrace. Now they were face to face and tightly bound together; if one or both of them fainted, it would be almost impossible to slip off the end of the rope.

This time in the darkness of the well, Jessica tried to concentrate on slowing her heart rate, and with her free hand rubbed slow circles on Aya's back. Down, down they went, into the water, up to their knees, their waists, their shoulders, until the cold darkness of the water engulfed them.

Shawn, Jason, D.J., and Darcelle stood in a tight huddle, their heads bowed, when a roar from the crowd jolted them out of prayer.

They looked up to see the limp forms of Jessica and Aya being pulled away from the rope. They disappeared amid the crowd of villagers, as loud, high-pitched warbles joined the deafening sound of the drums.

Shawn forced his way past one person after another, until he nearly tripped over Jessica, who was bent over Aya's thin form. As Shawn knelt beside the two of them, the chieftain's daughter was lying on her side, coughing a stream of water onto the dirt at Jessica's feet.

"Are you all right?" Shawn asked.

Jessica nodded tearfully. He took her into his arms, and she cried on his shoulder.

"I was so scared," Shawn told her.

She coughed. Shawn could feel her body shaking all over. "You're the one who said I should take more risks."

He knew she was trying to joke, but his answer was serious. "I take it back," he said. "I take it back."

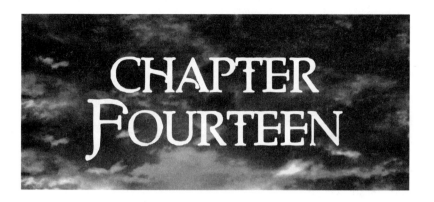

CHAPTER FOURTEEN

Thoroughly soaked, Jessica bent and helped Aya to her feet as everyone crowded around them. She took Aya's hands in hers intending to untie the rope that still bound her hands together. The tight circle around them parted and the chief man—Aya's father—appeared, tall and stern beside them.

Jessica embraced Aya tightly and they faced him together. His expression was unsmiling, but Jessica thought she detected a softening in his features. She was trying hard to think of what to say to him when Duane Cunningham appeared, holding one of the Dogon Bibles they had brought to the village just a few days earlier—though it seemed now like ages ago.

"Joe!" Duane called. "Joe, I need you!"

Moments later Joe called back, just before he appeared, threading through the tightly-packed clot of people.

"Joe," Duane said, "I need you to translate for me. It's very important."

Joe nodded in agreement, and Duane turned to face the chieftain.

Duane opened the Bible in his hand and held it open near the beginning, as he told the chief man—and everyone around who listened raptly—that "what just happened here in this village is the story of this book in action." He paused every few phrases, so Joe could translate his words into Dogon, telling the chief the story of Abraham, who took his son Isaac to a high mountain to sacrifice him as an act of repentance and obedience to God.

"When Abraham arrived at the mountain where the sacrifice was to be made," Duane continued, "he left his servants and the donkey behind and climbed the mountain with his son. There he built an altar, stacked wood on it, tied his son's hands, and laid the boy on the altar. But just as he was lifting his knife in the air to kill his son—whom he loved—an angel spoke to him and said, 'Do not lay a hand on the boy.'

"Abraham spared his son, and immediately a ram appeared in a bush nearby, tangled by his horns. So Abraham sacrificed the ram instead, and God was pleased with him."

Duane turned the pages of the book as he continued, finding pages he was pretty sure corresponded to the last chapters of the Gospel of John. He told how many years later, after men and women had done many wrong things, year after year, God sent another substitute. Only this time, it was his own Son, whose name was Jesus. He told the chief—and the entire crowd—how Jesus was born as a baby in a small village and lived a sinless life. "And then," Duane said, "he gave his life as a sacrifice, and endured the terrible punishment we deserved for all the wrong things we have done—we, and our children." He glanced meaningfully at Aya and Jessica.

"Now," Duane concluded, "none of us need to fear the curse of evil any longer. Jesus took our punishment, like Jessica did for Aya, so that we could be forgiven and cleansed—so we could please God with the rest of our lives."

Joe stopped abruptly in his translation.

"What's wrong?" Duane asked.

Joe wrinkled his forehead. "It is the word 'forgiveness.' They do not know that word."

Darcelle stepped forward. "Tell him it means, 'cleansing without punishment.'"

Joe nodded, turned to the head man, and offered the translation. The chieftain nodded seriously, and Joe finished the translation of Duane's final words.

Aya's father turned his glance from Duane's face and looked at his daughter. Then he fastened his gaze on Jessica. He reached out and took the Dogon Bible from Duane's hands. He bowed his head over the page and read with obvious difficulty. When he lifted his gaze, he again looked at Jessica. He spoke.

Joe translated, "He asks, 'This book is true?'"

Jessica looked from the head man to Joe. "Is he asking *me*?"

"Yes," Joe said. "You."

Jessica looked back at the man. She met his searching gaze, and nodded. "Tell him, 'Yes, absolutely.'"

† † † † † † †

"How—HOW—," stammered Ratsbane, his frog body quivering all over and his ant head lolling back and forth as if it might soon roll off his shoulders and onto the cavern floor. "How did this happen?"

He stared with glassy black eyes at the scene on the giant plasma screen. His arms hung limply at his sides, and the remote control in his right hand sparked and smoked, its circuits hopelessly fried. Nefarius skulked nearby, sharpening his good tusk with a tiny nail file.

"How did this happen?" Ratsbane repeated.

"I'll tell you how it happened, you pathetic bobble-headed toad," barked Nefarius.

Ratsbane suddenly straightened. "What did you call me?"

"You heard what I called you," the larger demon answered. "And I will call you worse, because you're finished!"

"Finished?" Ratsbane croaked. "I'm not finished. This is a setback, yes, but I am Ratsbane, the mighty demon winner of the Ignoble Prize!"

"Give me a break, you sorry piece of slime. Your whole Project TruthTwister is a failure, at least among these kids. But don't worry your bloated insect head about that. Under my leadership, Project TruthTwister will corrupt and destroy far more humans, youth groups, and churches than your wildest dreams could ever have achieved!"

A series of loud, disgusting bellows rose from Ratsbane's frog belly and he spat them out one after another. Finally, his bile exhausted, he waved the ruined remote in Nefarius's face. "What are you smoking, you freak show refugee? You could never lead Project TruthTwister! You don't have the brains."

"I have the brains to outsmart you," Nefarius countered. "I had the brains to turn the group back to the village, didn't I?"

"Turn the group—" Ratsbane sputtered. "What are you talking about?"

"It was genius, really," Nefarius said. "All I had to do was tell Rankmeat to make sure the drumming started before the Americans' van was out of sight." He grinned broadly, his broken tusk making him look ridiculous instead of intelligent.

Ratsbane stared uncomprehendingly at his underdemon. "I don't understand."

"Of course you don't. That's the only smart thing I've heard you say. Ever." Nefarius grunted and stomped toward Ratsbane, who was a fraction of his size. "You've assumed that because I'm big, I'm stupid. I've let you believe that, but I've always been waiting, waiting for my chance to humiliate you, bring down your project, and take your command. All I had to do was make sure that vanload of kids heard the drumming start, and I knew they would turn back."

"How did you know that?" Ratsbane said, his tone poisoned with hatred.

"Because, you fool, you had already let them get too far down the path of knowing the enemy and learning his ways! You're the most pathetic excuse for a demon of hell I've ever seen!"

"Wait!" Ratsbane protested, as Nefarius picked up a filthy bucket from the floor by the cavern door and strode still closer to Ratsbane. "That wasn't my fault! I—"

Nefarius swung the bucket against the side of Ratsbane's bulbous head. "Tell that to your foreman on sludge detail."

"Slu—" Ratsbane sputtered. "I will *not* be put on sludge detail. I'm Ratsbane! I'm the genius of Subsector 477! I'm the brains behind Project TruthTwister! I'm the recipient of the Ignoble Prize!"

Nefarius clamped a heavy gorilla paw on Ratsbane's head and steered him toward the exit. "Yeah, yeah," he said. "And you're the newest drudge in the Chernobyl Sulfur Pits. Congratulations."

† † † † † † †

The chief man of the village studied Jessica as Joe translated her answer to his question. He handed the Dogon Bible to Joe and in one stride closed the distance between him and his daughter.

For the first time, Jessica thought she detected mercy in his eyes as he looked at Aya. Her head was bowed, but when he reached out and lifted her hands, which were still bound together, she looked at him. He nodded solemnly and untied her hands, letting the rope drop to the ground at their feet.

Then the chieftain turned back to face Duane and Joe. He looked at Duane as he spoke.

Joe looked back and forth between the two men, but he did not relay the chief's words to Duane. Instead, he looked at the chief man and said something that sounded like a question, lifting the Bible the chief had given him just moments earlier.

The chieftain spoke again. He seemed to be using much the same words as before but spoke more forcefully this time. Joe nodded and turned to Duane with the hint of a smile on his face.

Joe lifted the Bible. "The head man of this village asks to barter with you for as many copies of this book as he can obtain."

Duane looked at Joe then at the chief man. He opened his mouth to speak.

"Wait!" Shawn interrupted. He left Jessica's side for the first time since her ordeal and whispered something in Duane's ear. Duane smiled and nodded, and Shawn stepped back beside Jessica.

"Tell him," Duane said, "that we will be pleased to ship them as many Dogon Bibles as they want in exchange for the village's hospitality . . . until the school we started is under roof." When he finished, he flashed a tiny smile in Shawn's direction.

Joe translated, and the chief man stared at Duane. Then, slowly, almost imperceptibly, he nodded. A moment later, he uttered a gruff syllable, turned and, with a dignified air, strutted away.

The entire Westcastle group watched him go in silent amazement. When he was gone, they erupted in laughter, cheers, and tears—Jessica most of all.

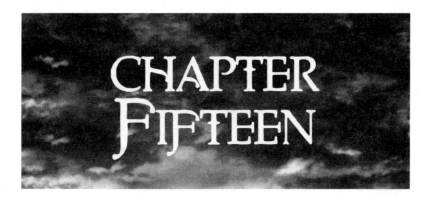

CHAPTER FIFTEEN

As the crowd around the well dispersed, Shawn stayed close to Jessica and was surprised that she didn't seem to mind.

"Guess you should change your clothes," he said.

"In this heat?" she answered. "They'll be dry before I can get my bag out of the van."

"Can I ask you a question?" he asked, as they walked slowly toward the van.

"You just did," she joked.

"How did you do that?" he asked.

She knew he referred to the ordeal she just went through. "I don't know," she said with a shrug. "Well, I guess I do. Sort of. It's just—I don't think I can explain it." They walked in silence for a few moments and then saw that the others were already pulling bags out of Joe's van. "It was like, when I was going down into the well the first time, I knew that there was no way I could do it. I knew if I was going to survive, I just had to give in."

"Give in?" Shawn asked.

She frowned, looking frustrated at her inability to express herself. "You know how most of the time we want God to do things our way? Like, we pray for him to make someone fall in love with us or get us a good grade on a test or whatever?"

Shawn shrugged. "Sure," he said.

"Well, I realized last night that's pretty much how I live my life. I had an experience—." She thought of telling Shawn about the old woman, but she avoided the idea for the moment. "I had an experience that showed me a lot and," she paused, "well, when I finally laid down to go to sleep last night, I prayed. I asked God to teach me what he was really like, and—this is going to sound weird—but to help me cooperate with his Holy Spirit to make him more and more at home in my life. I guess I kind of gave in to him in a new way.

"So," she continued, "when I was being lowered down into that well, I felt like I was giving in to whatever it was he wanted to show me or teach me—or maybe, I thought, use me to teach Aya. There's one more thing that's kind of strange," Jessica paused as if she wasn't sure she should say more. "I don't know what you'll make of this, but I'll tell you anyway. When we were being let down into the water, I felt strongly that someone else was with us—someone powerful and strong who was protecting us. I was scared in a way, but in another way this—this presence made me feel that he would protect me and make things come out okay, no matter what happened. It's hard to explain . . . The best I can say is that I suddenly understood how those three young Hebrew men must have felt when that fourth person appeared with them in the fire that was meant to burn them up."

"Wow," Shawn said in absolute wonder. He thought of his prayer for her as she descended into the well—that God would protect her like he protected those Hebrews. He felt a thrill run up his spine and couldn't speak for a moment. They had stopped walking and were standing not far from the van. The roof of the vehicle was already empty of luggage.

"If I hadn't had the experience last night," she said, "I know I couldn't have done it. I would have been even more scared; I would have been afraid that God wanted to hurt me the way my father used to hurt me. I wouldn't have been able to believe that God would be there with me in the well like he was with those Hebrew boys in the fire. I wouldn't have thought that he could actually get me through it. Because I knew he loves me and wants good things for me, I was able just to give in to him and say, basically, 'Okay, God, I'm going to do this with your help, so you've got to get me through it.' And he did."

Shawn was studying Jessica's face, an expression of surprise on his. "You never told me your father hurt you."

Jessica nodded. "Well," she said, "maybe I can now." She thought for a moment about the old woman and her experience of the previous night. She took Shawn's hand in hers. "In fact," she said, "I want you to come with me right now. I want to introduce you to somebody."

✝✝✝✝✝✝✝

(THE INSIDE STORY)
The Word and the Spirit

Jessica may not know it, but the experience she told Shawn about—the strength and comfort she received in her ordeal in the well—depicts the way it's supposed to happen for all of us. It is a portrayal of the power that results when we discover the truth in God's Word and yield to the influence of his Holy Spirit in order to live out the things his Word shows us, commands us, and teaches us.

When we discover God's Word as an open door to his heart, a way to know him better, what we learn of his love draws us to open ourselves to the intimate, personal relationship he offers. He can then enable us to do things we would not otherwise be able to do. The Bible says, "By his divine power, God has given us everything we need for living a godly life . . . He has given us great and precious promises. These are the promises that enable you to share his divine nature and escape the world's corruption caused by human desires" (2 Peter 1:3-4).

When Jessica met the old woman in the middle of the night, her eyes were opened to see that her image of God, her heavenly Father, had come partly out of her own past hurts and current fears. She thought that God, her heavenly Father, was much like her earthly father—that he was always ready to punish her for being a bad girl. When she discovered the truth about God's love for her—as God revealed it and wrote in his Word, the Bible—that truth transformed her because, as the Bible says, "The word of God is alive and powerful" (Hebrews 4:12).

What happened the next morning shows something else. Reading the Word—and even understanding it—is not enough all by itself. If we're going to experience all God wants for us, we also need the Holy Spirit to do what Jesus promised—to be an indwelling presence "who leads into all truth . . . He will teach you everything and will remind you of everything I have told you" (John 14:17, 26).

That's what happened the next morning with Jessica. She did not have the wisdom or strength in herself to jump up on that rope and endure the terrifying ordeal of sharing Aya's punishment. But—having learned the truth about her heavenly Father and his love for her—she was ready when the Holy Spirit reminded her of that truth the next morning. She was able to rely on God to empower her for all she had to face.

That can happen in each one of us—perhaps not in so dramatic a way—every day of our lives. While the Holy Spirit enters your life at the moment you surrender to God and accept Jesus as Savior and Lord, the Holy Spirit is not someone you are to simply experience once in your life. He is a person who wants to live in and through your life to produce the kind of life you were meant to live—a Christlike life. "The Holy Spirit produces this kind of fruit in our lives," the Bible says, "love, joy, peace, patience, kindness, goodness, faithfulness, gentleness, and self-control . . . Since we are living by the Spirit, let us follow the Spirit's leading in every part of our lives" (Galatians 5:22-23, 25). In other words, the Holy Spirit's job is to make Jesus Christ more and more at home in your heart as you trust in him (Ephesians 3:17), until—more and more—Christ's patience will replace your impatience, his peace will replace your anxiety, his love will replace your self-centeredness, his purity will replace your impurity, his life will become your life, conforming you "to the image of His Son" (Romans 8:29, NASB).

So how can you "be filled with the Holy Spirit" (Ephesians 5:18)? It involves a process of "giving in," as Jessica put it, to the Holy Spirit's guidance. It involves not only reading the Bible, but praying that God will reveal more of himself to you in what you read. It involves not only asking God, as Jessica said, "for him to make someone fall in love with us, or get us a good grade on a test," but surrendering yourself to his plans for your day and his will for your life.

Letting the Holy Spirit fill you is an essential ingredient in the power-filled Christian life. Letting him "teach you everything" and "remind you of everything [Jesus has] told you" (John 14:26) is absolutely indispensable if you want to discover the truth and hope to make Christ more and more at home in your life. We encourage you to ask your pastor for guidance in discovering and experiencing the "divine power" that gives us "everything we need for living a godly life" (2 Peter 1:3).

† † † † † † †

Jessica led Shawn past the girls' hut, where Liz, Darcelle, Sarah, and Alison were happily unpacking and chattering away about the morning's dramatic events. She led him along the short, twisting path she had taken the night before when she had followed the old woman's strange humming and the light of her tiny fire. A moment later, however, she stood with Shawn at the edge of the village beyond the last hut in that direction.

She looked around them with a confused expression on her face. "I don't understand," she said.

"What's wrong?" Shawn asked.

Jessica twirled, almost like a ballet dancer, making sure of her orientation. She retraced her steps and stood where the old woman's hut was supposed to be.

"Will you tell me what's going on?" Shawn said.

Jessica shook her head then slowly told Shawn the story of leaving her hut and meeting the old woman. She recapped for him almost their whole conversation, including every detail she could remember, from the woman's toothless smile to the way she poked and stirred the embers in the fire.

"I thought it was a dream," she said.

"Looks like it was," Shawn offered.

She shook her head vigorously. "Until this morning. When I hung on that rope with Aya, I saw her standing in the crowd. She held up her hands to me, like this." She demonstrated, tenting her hands together in a praying position, and holding them tightly together at the wrists. "I thought at first she was telling me to pray—and maybe she was—but the way she held her hands together at the wrists reminded me that Aya's hands were tied together, and that I could use that to keep us both from sliding off the rope and into the well if we passed out."

"So . . . you saw the woman . . . who lived in a hut that's no longer here?"

Jessica threw up her hands. "I know it sounds crazy, but I—look, I sat right here." She pointed to where she remembered sitting the previous night. What she saw choked off her next words. She stared at the ground.

"What?" Shawn asked. "What is it?"

Jessica lifted her gaze to his face. She smiled and pointed. "See those little black smudges in the dirt?"

Shawn nodded. He could see what looked like the remains of a tiny fire. "Yeah," he said.

She looked back at the sooty circle on the ground. "See the stick? With the blackened tip?"

"Yeah," he said.

"She was here," Jessica said, firmly. "Whoever she was, she was here."

"But the hut—"

She shrugged. "Maybe she was a dream. Maybe not," she said. "I just know she was here for me . . . and God was, too.

Jessica and Shawn were headed back toward the girls' hut when Aya appeared in their path.

"Hi," Jessica said. She was amazed at the sudden incredible depth of love she felt for this girl.

Aya fastened her bright eyes on Jessica, and they flowed with tears. She spoke rapidly, a string of words in her language that neither Jessica nor Shawn could understand.

Jessica fully understood Aya's next action. She extended her arms in Jessica's direction. Draped across her fingers was Jessica's necklace. She nodded, clearly indicating her desire to return the necklace.

Jessica's own eyes filled with tears. She took the necklace, unhooked the clasp, and gently wrapped it around Aya's neck.

The chieftain's daughter shook her head adamantly, but Jessica laid her hand on the necklace's teardrop pendant as it sparkled against the girl's dark skin. She said, "No, please. I want you to have it."

Jessica returned Aya's adoring gaze and hugged her new friend tightly.

EPILOGUE

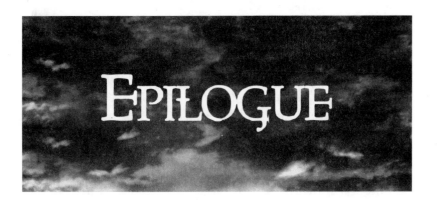

Jessica's online journal

i just got back from africa late last night. Actually, it was this morning. what an unbelievable trip. i'm not even sure i can understand everything that happened, much less explain it. but i know God— i mean, really, really know him—like never before. i know him for who he really is, not for who i thought he was or made him up to be in my own little mind. and for the first time in my life, I think I'm actually experiencing when the bible says something like, as you get to know him better, he becomes more and more at home in your heart, until you start acting more and more like him. or something like that. but that's what it's been like since my adventure in the well. i'll write more about that later. right now i'm still exhausted.

on the flight home, sarah asked me if it was hard to leave africa without my grandma's necklace. i told her, no, you'd think it would be. but i'm so excited for aya— i'll write more about her, too, but she's an african girl who actually prayed to receive Christ before we left. i've never been so excited in my life as i was when that happened. and i feel like— i don't even know how to explain this, but— i feel like i've figured out a whole new purpose for my life. before it was just trying to make God happy so he wouldn't get mad at me and have to punish me, but it's not like that at all anymore. now i know that i can actually become more and more like Jesus, as i read the bible and yield to the Holy Spirit in my life . . . i'm still figuring all that out, but duane and liz and darcelle have already been helping me with that.

oh, one more thing before i sign off. i think this trip to africa has changed shawn, too. we're not back together—yet—but he told me how he'd been thinking that he needed something in his life . . . and that something was always me, in his mind. but he told me in africa that he still thinks i'm incredible and all that, and still hopes we'll be a couple again, sometime. he said he's realized that he's not yet the kind of guy i deserve until he gets to know God better and becomes more like Christ. he said he wants to take things slow when we get back home, so he can focus on doing that, and then we'll see if God wants us to be a couple again someday. i couldn't believe it when he said that! it made me think, maybe shawn IS the kind of guy i deserve! :)

Guidelines for Interpreting and Applying Scripture

These three simple steps will help you to discover the objective truth of God's message to you in the Bible. If you follow these steps, keeping your mind open to hear what God is actually saying instead of what you may have been feeling inside about him, you will come to see him for who he really is. Don't rely on the distorted picture of him that you inadvertently create from your own emotions and experiences.

Ask "What Does It Say?"

Whenever you read the Bible, you need to "see it" for what it says. You need to understand what is in a passage. You do this by running Scripture through a six-part grid represented by these questions: Who? What? When? Where? Why? and How?

1. *Who?* This question helps determine who the personalities are in the passage. Ask: Who is talking? Who is the passage talking about?

2. *What?* This question helps determine the subject, message, or atmosphere of a passage. Ask: What is happening in the passage? What did the people in the passage do? What caused that? What is the theme?

3. *When?* This question helps determine time elements of a passage. Ask: When did it happen? When will it happen? When can it happen?

4. *Where?* This question helps determine the location in which a passage happens. Ask: Where did it happen? Where are the people going? Where will it take place?

5. *Why?* This question helps determine the underlying message or reasons outlined in a passage. Ask: Why did the writer say that? Why did the character do that? Why did the character go there? Why will this happen?

6. *How?* This question helps us determine the process involved in a passage. Ask: How did it happen? How was it supposed to happen? How will it happen? Under what circumstances will the message or promise of the passage come true?

You may not be able to answer all six questions in every passage, but by asking and answering as many as possible, you will come to understand what the Word of God is saying.

Ask "What Does It Mean?"

Whenever we read God's Word, we need to "know it" for what it means. This is where many of us mess up, like back in chapter two, when Jessica asked her girls' Bible study: "What do those verses mean *to you*?"

Understanding the significance of a portion of Scripture *is not* the same as asking, "What does it *mean to me or you?*" Understanding Scripture is not "a matter of one's own interpretation." The words of the Bible have an objective meaning of their own—the meaning God intended. When you read a passage of the Bible, you need to ask, "What is the objective meaning or significance of this passage?" and then let the Scripture interpret that for you. This is where the Bible study tools and techniques below are helpful:

1. *Study the context.* Scripture must be understood in context. Giving careful consideration to the verses and chapters that go before and after a particular portion of Scripture is necessary to understand the objective meaning of the passage. Understanding the cultural context of a passage is also crucial. Many parts of the Bible can be confusing unless one understands the cultural setting in which they were spoken or written. Answering the detail questions—Who? What? When? Where? Why? How?—of a passage will go a long way in understanding the cultural context of a passage. Reference books such as study Bibles, Bible commentaries, encyclopedias, or atlases are helpful in discovering the cultural context of a passage.

2. *Study the words and phrases.* Scripture is rich in meaning when we look at individual words and phrases that are used in specific ways. Several reference tools can help you understand what words and phrases mean:

   - *Concordances.* Use a concordance—an alphabetized list of words used in the Bible—to help you find other places where the word or phrase is used in Scripture. This will allow you to compare how the specific word or phrase is used in various contexts. Many concordances include the original Hebrew and Greek words for the English translation, and some understanding of the original meanings of words and phrases in a text often shed light on a passage's meaning.

   - *Cross-references.* Many Bibles have marginal cross-references that allow you to go from one verse to another that is similar or that contains the same word or phrase. Comparing cross-references can help you understand the objective, original meaning of a word or phrase.

   - *Study Bibles.* Study Bibles are a rich source of background information about words, phrases, characters, prophecies, historical context, diagrams, and other valuable information that will help you understand the meaning of a passage.

- *Bible dictionaries.* Bible dictionaries can help even the novice Bible student understand the meaning of words used in Scripture.
- *Other Bible translations and paraphrases.* A dynamic way of understanding a passage better is reading it in a variety of translations or paraphrases. As you do this, take care to identify which Bibles are true translations (translated from the original languages) and which are paraphrases (based on English translations, for example, *The Message*). Translations will be more accurate for word study; paraphrases are often used for devotional purposes.

3. *Read what scholars have written about the passage.* Reading what Bible scholars have written in commentaries about various passages can illumine even the most straightforward verses. You can benefit from the exhaustive study many of the commentators have made of the Scripture. It is also helpful to compare the writings of the church fathers and great Christian commentators of the past with the analyses of more modern scholars.

By making use of sound Bible study techniques and the excellent study tools available to us today, every Christian can learn the objective meaning of the biblical text. Of course, there is diversity within the church on various points of theology, forms of worship, and church standards and practices, but there are only a few scriptural passages that are not clearly understandable.

Ask "How Does It Apply?"

Whenever we encounter the truth of God's Word, we need to also "experience it" in our own lives and relationships.

At least three categories of questions can help you to experience the truth:

1. *Identify the truth.* How is this truth of Scripture to be experienced in my relationship with God and/or others? What is this truth supposed to look like, sound like, and act like in my life?

2. *Know the hindrances to the truth.* What hinders me from trusting Christ to live out this truth in my life? What sins, self-centered attitudes, expressions of self-reliance, or other things might hinder me from experiencing this truth? What will I do with these hindrances?

3. *Commit to experiencing the truth.* What practical steps can I take to know God more and make Christ more at home in my heart? How can I put the truth of Scripture into practice? How can I allow Christ to live his life through me? What is the first step I must take? Whom will I ask to pray with me about making the truth of Scripture an experienced reality in my life?

Again, it's important to emphasize the goal of reading and studying the Bible. We shouldn't study the Bible simply to know what Scripture says. We should read God's words for a relational purpose—to know him, to understand his ways, and to allow him to live his life in and through our lives.

When we seek to discover what God's Word says, what it means, and how it applies to our lives—and can be experienced in our lives and relationships—then we open new doors to a passionate, exciting relationship with God . . . and with others.

APPENDIX B

Evidence for the Reliability of the Bible

Repeatedly throughout history, the evidence has given us assurance that God's Word has been recorded exactly, relayed accurately, and reinforced externally. The three points summarized below will show you that when we hold the Bible in our hands and read it, we can know that it is an accurate revelation of God—the God who wants us to know him. The evidence shows us that we can know that it is reliable. We can trust the information it contains and know that it is not only accurate but is worth sharing with others.

1. **God's Word Has Been Recorded Exactly**
   The overwhelming weight of scholarship supports the conclusion that the Bible's accounts of Jesus' life, the history of the early church, and the letters that form the bulk of the New Testament were accurate:

   - In fact, Luke (one of the New Testament authors) said that the people who "have attempted to write about what had taken place among us . . . *received their information from those who had been eyewitnesses* and servants of God's word from the beginning, and they passed it on to us" (Luke 1:1-2, GWT, italics added).

- Other New Testament writers, like John and Peter, testified that they had observed with their own eyes the things they reported:

  "The one who saw this is an eyewitness." (John 19:35, GWT)

  "We proclaim to you what we ourselves have actually seen and heard." (1 John 1:3)

  "We witnessed his majesty with our own eyes." (2 Peter 1:16, GWT)

- The speakers and writers of the Bible accounts made frequent appeals to their audience, along the lines of, "If you don't believe me, check out the facts for yourself!" (See Acts 2:32; 3:15; 13:31; 1 Corinthians 15:3-6.)

(More on this area of evidence, known as the internal evidence test of the Old and New Testaments, is documented in chapters 3, 4, and 21 of the book *The New Evidence That Demands a Verdict*.)

2. **God's Word Has Been Relayed Accurately**

The overwhelming weight of evidence also affirms that the Bible has been accurately relayed through the centuries to the present day. In other words, when you pick up a Bible and read it today, you can be absolutely confident that you are reading the words substantially as they were recorded thousands of years ago.

Historians evaluate the textual reliability of ancient literature according to two standards: (1) what the time interval is between the original and the earliest copy; and (2) how many manuscripts are available. The chart on page 163 lists some of the most reliable works of ancient literature and history:

Textual Reliability Standards Applied to Classical Literature

AUTHOR	BOOK	DATE WRITTEN	EARLIEST COPIES	TIME GAP	NO. OF COPIES
Homer	*Iliad*	800 B.C.	c. 400 B.C.	c. 400 yrs.	643
Herodotus	*History*	480–425 B.C.	c. A.D. 900	c. 1,350 yrs.	8
Thucydides	*History*	460–400 B.C.	c. A.D. 900	c. 1,300 yrs.	8
Plato		400 B.C.	c. A.D. 900	c. 1,300 yrs.	7
Demosthenes		300 B.C.	c. A.D. 1100	c. 1,400 yrs.	200
Caesar	*Gallic Wars*	100–44 B.C.	c. A.D. 900	c. 1,000 yrs.	10
Livy	*History of Rome*	59 B.C.–A.D. 17	4th cent. (partial) mostly 10th cent.	c. 400 yrs. c. 1,000 yrs.	1 partial 19 copies
Tacitus	*Annals*	A.D. 100	c. A.D. 1100	c. 1,000 yrs.	20
Pliny Secundus	*Natural History*	A.D. 61–113	c. A.D. 850	c. 750 yrs.	7

By comparison, the New Testament stands alone. It has no equal. No other book of the ancient world can even approach the reliability of the New Testament, as the table on page 165 shows.

The evidence for the reliability of the Old and New Testaments is not only convincing and compelling but also a clear and praiseworthy indication of how God lovingly supervised its accurate transmission so that he might preserve for us—and our children—all the blessings that come from knowing him and obeying his Word.

3. God's Word Has Been Reinforced Externally

The Bible's accuracy and reliability have also been reinforced through external evidence. A routine criterion in examining the reliability of an historical document is whether *other* historical material confirms or denies the internal testimony of the document itself. Historians ask, "What sources, apart from the literature under examination, substantiate its accuracy and reliability?"

In the case of the Bible, this external evidence adds a coda to the masterpiece God has composed in creating, conveying, and confirming the Scriptures that reveal him to us.

In all of history, the Bible is by far the most widely referenced and quoted book. Consider just the few following facts:

- The New Testament alone is so extensively quoted in the ancient manuscripts of non-biblical authors that all twenty-seven books from Matthew through Revelation could be reconstructed virtually word-for-word from those sources.
- The writings of early Christians like Eusebius (A.D. 339) in his *Ecclesiastical History 111.39* and Irenaeus (A.D. 180) in his *Against Heresies 111* reinforce the text of the apostle John's writings.

Textual Reliability Standards Applied to the Bible

AUTHOR	BOOK	DATE WRITTEN	EARLIEST COPIES	TIME GAP	NO. OF COPIES
John	New Testament	A.D. 50-100	c. A.D. 130	+50 yrs.	Fragments
The rest of the New Testament authors			c. A.D. 200 (books)	100 yrs.	
			c. A.D. 250 (most of N.T.)	150 yrs.	
			c. A.D. 325 (complete N.T.)	225 yrs.	+5,600 Greek mss.
			c. A.D. 366–384 (Latin Vulgate trans.)	284 yrs.	
			c. A.D. 400–500 (other trans.)	400 yrs.	+19,000 trans. mss.
			TOTALS	50–400 yrs.	+24,900 mss.

- Clement of Rome (A.D. 95), Ignatius (A.D. 70–110), Polycarp (A.D. 70–156), and Titian (A.D. 170) offer external confirmation of other New Testament accounts.
- Non-Christian historians such as the first-century Roman historian Tacitus (A.D. 55–117) and the Jewish historian Josephus (A.D. 37–100) confirm the substance of some scriptural accounts.
- Over and over again through the centuries, archaeological discoveries have confirmed once-doubted parts of the biblical account:
    - the confirmation that writing existed long before the time of Moses;
    - the existence of King David (whom radical scholars once thought was a mythical figure);
    - the existence of King Belshazzar (Daniel 5);
    - the existence of Pontius Pilate and Caiaphas, who figured in the gospel accounts of Jesus' trial and crucifixion;
    - the existence of Lysanias the Tetrarch (Luke 3:1) during the time of Jesus.

These and other outside sources substantiate the accuracy of the biblical record like that of no other book in history. (For more information on the confirmation of the Bible's reliability in extrabiblical sources, see chapters 3 and 4 of *The New Evidence That Demands a Verdict*.)

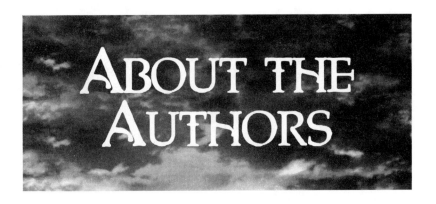

About the Authors

Josh McDowell is an internationally known speaker, author, and traveling representative of Campus Crusade for Christ. He has authored or coauthored more than sixty books including *More Than a Carpenter* and *The New Evidence That Demands a Verdict*. Josh and his wife, Dottie, have four children and live in California.

Bob Hostetler is a writer, editor, pastor, and speaker. He has written numerous books, including *Beyond Belief to Convictions* (coauthored with Josh McDowell) and *American Idols: The Worship of the American Dream*. He and his wife, Robin, have two children and live in southwestern Ohio.